FATAL

DECEPTION

AN EMERALD CITY THRILLER

AUDREY J.
COLE

RAINIER PUBLISHING

ISBN: 9798662945449

CHAPTER ONE

Andrea pulled aside the plum velvet curtain and peeked through the rain-streaked window of the Gothic Tudor mansion. In the moonlight, she could see the Ferrari still parked in the circular drive two stories below. It was her only chance of escape.

She let go of the heavy fabric and stepped away from the window. As she crept toward the door, she glanced at her roommate already asleep in the large, four-poster bed. Andrea pulled slowly on the solid wood door, but there was no stopping the loud creak that came from the ancient English oak.

"Where are you going?"

Andrea turned to see Violet sitting up in bed. Her heart raced. "Oh. Just to the bathroom. I'll be right back."

Andrea watched her roommate lie back against her pillow before she stepped into the hall. The hall was dimly lit from the lights that remained on downstairs. All the girls had retired to their rooms. The only ones still awake were their leader and his dinner guest, the CEO of a tech giant that started in Seattle.

Andrea smoothed the base of her short silk nightgown

when she reached the top of the wooden staircase. She looked down at her bare legs as she tiptoed down the stairs. As she reached the bottom of the stairs, she could hear laughter in the library.

She glanced at the solid oak doors at the castle's main entrance, knowing she couldn't use them for her escape. The security camera on the outside would give her away immediately. She knew there was also a guard roaming the perimeter, but she'd have to avoid being seen.

She stepped off the stairs onto the herringbone floor. She moved past two medieval knights propped next to the staircase, exported from Wales by the castle's original owner, when she heard the voice of their dinner guest.

"Thank you so much for having me. I better get back to the city," said the tech CEO.

The door to the library opened, flooding the mansion's grand entrance with light. Andrea ran toward the rear of the home on the balls of her feet.

"There's just one more thing I'd like to show you before you go." There was no mistaking the deep voice of their leader before she slipped inside the slightly ajar door to the butler's pantry.

Andrea ran through the narrow space toward the door that opened to the rear of the property. She glanced behind her shoulder before turning the knob. She looked in both directions before stepping onto the damp concrete patio. There was no guard in sight.

The rear of the estate's exterior was softly lit by an occasional Gothic lamppost. She ran to the right, stopping in her tracks when she saw the outline of the guard step out from beside the massive structure. She looked down at her white silk gown, realizing she stuck out like a ghost in the night. She should've changed into dark clothes, but what would she have said if she'd got caught before she left the castle?

The guard stopped as a familiar male voice came over her radio.

"Camilla, could you please let Rachelle out the front gate in a few minutes? She's just leaving."

"Sure thing," Andrea heard Camilla reply before she disappeared around the side of the house. Andrea turned and sprinted barefoot across the cold patio. She could only hope she'd make it to the Ferrari before being seen.

Heart pumping, she rounded the dark corner. She pushed herself to run faster along the wet grass until she reached the front of the grand home.

She was out of breath when she reached the circular driveway. The Ferrari was still parked in the drive, in front of the sculpted fountain. Andrea stood alone on the grounds of the large, gated compound for a brief moment before Camilla stepped out from the side of the castle. Camilla hummed to herself as she made her way across the lawn with her rifle slung over her shoulder. Andrea crouched behind the sports car and waited until Camilla's footsteps sounded on the paved drive. Andrea lifted her head above the roof of the Ferrari and watched Camilla stroll in the opposite direction.

She reached for the trunk, but her hand stilled an inch from the latch above the emblem of a silver prancing horse.

Their leader had made a comment when the tech CEO had arrived that there was no need to lock her car inside his gated estate. Hearing this had spurred Andrea's escape plan in her mind. But now she worried if he had only made the comment as a joke. Or as an excuse to brag about his private estate's security. Andrea would surely be caught—and punished—if her attempt to open the trunk set off the sports car's alarm.

But she had no choice. She couldn't stay here any longer. She pressed her fingers beneath the trunk latch and pulled. The rear window lifted without a noise. She took a last glance toward the castle before she climbed inside the trunk. She lay on her side with her knees pulled to her chest, surprised at the ample room inside the rear of the Ferrari.

"Thank you so much again for coming."

A knot formed in her throat at the sound of voices on the castle's front steps.

"I do hope you'll consider joining us," he schmoozed. "I think you'll gain great empowerment from the organization."

The Ferrari's rear window stuck straight in the air. Andrea grabbed the base of the window and pulled. She tried to be firm enough for it to latch, yet not create any noise. It closed with a soft click. Andrea hoped it was quiet enough not to be detected from the mansion's front steps.

Rachelle's heeled boots clacked against the concrete drive as she neared the Ferrari. Andrea lay her head against the felt-like carpet in the base of the trunk and tried to control her breathing.

Had she shut the trunk completely? Had the tech CEO heard her?

She squeezed her eyes shut as the footsteps drew closer. Despite her best efforts, her breathing rate rapidly increased. She'd never done well in closed spaces. She knew climbing into the tight space wasn't going to be easy, but she'd forgotten the intensity of the fear now overtaking her body.

Andrea heard the driver's door open and felt the woman get in. Andrea felt her chest tighten as she heard the tech CEO rifle through her purse. What was she doing? A minute passed, and Andrea wondered if something had given away her presence. Was she texting their leader?

The driver's door shut seconds before she started the engine. Andrea exhaled as the sports car moved slowly down the long private drive. She clasped her hands tightly together to keep them from trembling. Her body shifted back and forth as the car stopped and waited for Camilla to open the gate.

After being there for so long, it seemed unthinkable that she could make a clean escape in the trunk of their dinner guest's Ferrari. Maybe her roommate had already told their leader how Andrea had gone to the bathroom and never returned. Maybe she'd been picked up on a security camera she was unaware of.

There seemed a million reasons why this would never work. She was sure, any minute, Camilla would open the trunk and drag her back to the mansion. Andrea held her breath until the Ferrari's engine revved and she felt the car turn onto the narrow, two-lane road in front of the compound.

For the next thirty minutes, Andrea kept waiting for the car to pull over, and to be dragged out of the trunk by their leader.

"You just made the ten-thirty," she heard the ferry worker say from inside the toll booth.

"Great," Rachelle said.

They were almost off the island. For the first time since she got in the trunk, Andrea believed she might actually get away.

The car pulled forward. A moment later, Andrea felt the car drive onto the ferry. The car stopped and Rachelle got out, closing the driver's door softly behind her. Andrea took the opportunity to readjust her position in the trunk while she was alone in the car.

She didn't dare get out on the ferry. Just in case they'd been followed. Plus, she had no money, no clothes aside from her nightgown, and she needed to get to the city.

Rachelle returned to her car and drove the Ferrari off the boat twenty minutes later. Time moved slowly even as the car sped down the freeway to downtown Seattle. Andrea's legs were starting to cramp from the tight space. Her heart had finally stopped racing once they reached the mainland, her claustrophobia overpowered by a relief of escaping the confines of the island.

The Ferrari's engine turned off and Andrea realized they'd parked. Her body tensed as she listened to the tech CEO get out of the sports car. Her heels clicked against the concrete as she walked past the rear of the car, but then grew softer with each step. Andrea waited a few minutes in silence before she pulled the trunk's emergency release lever.

The glass panel lifted with a soft hiss. Andrea climbed out slowly into the parking garage, stretching her cramped muscles as she stood. The garage was filled with cars, but no people.

She'd heard Rachelle mention her Belltown penthouse apartment over dinner, which would put her less than a mile of where she needed to go. Her bare feet were silent atop the cement as she scurried to the nearest stairwell.

Andrea wondered if it was a mistake not to get Rachelle's attention after she parked.

She flew down the stairs. There was only one person she could trust. Hopefully her sister hadn't moved from her downtown apartment in the two years Andrea had been at the castle. She never attempted any contact with the outside world while she was there.

She pushed open the heavy door onto the street when she reached the bottom. She ignored the stare from a passerby as she checked the cross streets. She was near the waterfront on the edge of Belltown, only about ten blocks from her sister's building.

She'd made it two blocks before she noticed the black SUV creeping along behind her. She knew it might be her imagination. Even if their leader knew she'd left with their dinner guest, he would've been at least one ferry behind them. *Right?*

Andrea watched the SUV speed ahead and parallel park ahead of her. The car quietly idled as she walked closer. The windows were tinted, making it impossible to see inside. But she swore she'd seen that car at the compound before. It looked identical to several black SUVs kept at the castle.

She turned onto the next street before she reached the car. She ran down the hill toward the lit up *PUBLIC MARKET* sign above Pike's Place that glowed a bright salmon in the night sky. She took a left onto the brick cobblestone street, seeing the sign that cars could only turn right.

The only cars on the street were parked on the side, and Andrea moved quickly along in the middle of the road. A vibration from tires turning onto the brick-paved street caused her to turn. The black SUV sped in the opposite direction before its brake lights flashed. The dark vehicle's tires screeched and its engine droned before it reversed in

Andrea's direction.

She turned and raced toward a stairwell where the street curved to the left. The rev of the SUV's engine grew louder the closer she got to the stairs. She didn't dare to turn around until she jumped onto the sidewalk and rounded the top of the stairwell. Her hand closed around the cold metal railing as the SUV braked a few feet from the curb. Andrea's foot scraped atop the cement when she tripped halfway down, but she caught herself before she fell.

She didn't hear any sounds from the SUV when she got to the bottom of the staircase. She didn't wait to listen if the SUV drove away or if the driver got out of the car. She ran down the enclosed alleyway and zig-zagged down more flights of concrete steps between buildings. It was too secluded for her to stay there. If the driver followed after her, there would be nowhere to hide. She needed somewhere between isolation and out in the open.

The Viaduct. The overpass adjacent to the Seattle waterfront would be the perfect place to provide shelter from their leader, or whomever he'd sent to retrieve her.

The stairs widened when she reached the bottom. She looked to her left and then to her right when she stepped onto the sidewalk. The Viaduct was gone! Andrea stood in the complete open across the street from the waterfront. She had an unobstructed view of the Ferris wheel, lit up a light fluorescent blue on the pier behind the Seattle Aquarium. She wondered how the giant elevated highway had disappeared in the two years she'd been gone. *Was there another earthquake?*

She didn't see the dark SUV lurking anywhere on the waterfront road, which was still busy at midnight. At least not yet. She crossed the street where there were more people to blend in with. She shivered from the cold breeze that came over the water onto her bare legs. It was the first time since she'd gotten out of the Ferrari that she'd noticed the cold.

The sidewalk was filled with large groups of teenage girls, most wearing matching t-shirts with *BILLIE EILISH* printed across the front. Andrea walked against the flow of the crowd, noticing many of the girls wore glow sticks around their necks. She checked the street again. A few cars and SUVs drove past, but none seemed to slow at the sight of her.

She moved farther up the street when she noticed a dark SUV parked against the curb. It was the same make and model as the one following her earlier. The engine was turned off, and she couldn't tell if there was anyone inside. She pushed herself between two girls to create more distance between herself and the SUV as she walked by.

"Excuse you!" one of the girls yelled.

Andrea moved faster, pushing through the crowd. She heard the SUV's engine start and she turned to see it creep forward, keeping with her pace. A car honked before overtaking the larger vehicle.

She grabbed hold of a girl's arm in line for Ivar's. "Please! Help me! That car is after me!"

The girl stepped back as an older woman shoved Andrea's arm away and gave her a threatening look.

"Don't touch my daughter." The woman turned her back to Andrea after stepping between her and the teenage girl.

"Just ignore her honey. She's probably on drugs."

Other people in line shot Andrea wary glances. She looked down at her tiny nightgown blowing in the night breeze. It barely covered the top of her skinny thighs. She probably did look like a drug user. Or prostitute. Or both.

Andrea moved through the Ivar's line as the patrons made a wide gap for her go through. She broke into a run, bumping into the occasional oncomer. The SUV pulled forward to keep up with her pace.

Her heart pounded. She needed to get off the street.

The SUV stopped for a red light and she knew this was her chance. She raced across the street, ignoring the judgmental stare from a man who crossed from the other side.

She ran a few steps up the hill before turning back, relieved to see the SUV still at the light, waiting for a few slow-moving pedestrians to finish crossing. But she wouldn't make it all the way to her sister's apartment before the SUV caught up to her.

She tucked into an alley on her left. It was dimly lit by only a couple lampposts. She caught her breath as she slowed her pace and saw there was a dumpster up ahead that she could hide behind.

The alley lit up from behind her. She turned and squinted from the blinding headlights of the SUV barreling toward her.

She sprinted toward the dumpster, which was still a ways up the alley. She saw an entrance to a parking garage ahead, but it was gated. She darted again for the dumpster.

The lights grew brighter. Andrea turned back a second before the bumper tore into her leg. She fell against the hood, rolling up to the windshield from the car's momentum. Pain ripped through her left leg as the side of her face slammed against the glass in front of the driver.

The SUV slammed on its brakes, sending Andrea off the

hood before she could see who was trying to run her down. She rolled onto the rough pavement of the alleyway. The SUV's engine roared as Andrea tried to push herself up from the ground.

She'd barely moved when the bright beams of the truck sped toward her for the final time. The betrayal she felt, after she'd devoted her life and given everything, was as strong as the force from the vehicle's impact.

CHAPTER TWO

Detective Tess Richards tried her best to suppress the tightening in her chest as she ascended the wooden steps. She'd been called to the address for a suspected double stabbing. It was only the second crime scene she'd been called to since she returned to homicide from her stint in missing persons. She looked out at Lake Washington in the distance when she reached the top of the stairs. The neighborhood was southeast of Seattle, known for its mix of pre- and post-war homes.

The narrow street was already lined with law enforcement vehicles. She'd passed her partner's unmarked Ford on her way to the house, along with her sergeant's SUV, and a patrol unit. A CSI van was pulling up to the curb. Another van from the local news station had set up camp on the edge of the crime scene tape. She was glad to have avoided them on her way inside.

Tess hoped her deep breath would soothe her anxiety as she stepped inside the newly remodeled home.

Her partner, Ben Suarez, stood over the body of an elderly man lying next to the kitchen table in a pool of blood. He waved her in his direction after she passed through the entryway. Tess swallowed hard and nodded at the two crime scene investigators who turned in her direction as she moved through the living room.

"This is our first victim, Scott McGraw, seventy-eight years old."

Tess examined the body while Suarez continued. He lay on his back on a woven rug in a mess of dark blood. A large gash through his left forearm looked to be a defensive wound. Using a gloved hand, Suarez lifted the man's blood-stained t-shirt, exposing multiple stab wounds. It was hard to see the exact number of entry wounds through all the congealed blood.

Tess squatted next to her partner, pushing thoughts of her brother's brutal murder out of her mind.

"I'm guessing there's even more entry wounds on his back, but we'll have to wait for the ME before we move him," Suarez said.

"Who found him?" Tess asked.

"The neighbor. He and Scott had plans to watch the Mariners game together. They're both widowers. The front door was unlocked, so when Scott didn't answer, the neighbor let himself in. According to the first responders, he was very distraught when they arrived." Suarez stood up. "I'm guessing he was killed in the early morning hours, but we'll see what the ME thinks when he gets here."

"And the second victim?" Tess asked.

"He was found on the back deck. He's Scott's thirty-seven-year-old son."

Tess stood and followed her partner out of the kitchen, careful not to step on any blood. More crime scene investigators began to fill the home in the time Tess had been there.

"This is also the son's listed address. He's been arrested twice for drug possession. According to the neighbor who called 9-1-1, he checked out early from a crystal meth rehab program a few days ago and his father refused to let him live back at home until he finished the program. Unlike his father, he doesn't look to have any defensive wounds. Could be a murder-suicide."

Tess could feel the attack coming on as soon as she stepped through the open sliding door. The man lay on his back and a butcher knife protruded from the left side of his chest.

Suarez continued to talk while a crime scene investigator took photos of the body, but Tess couldn't hear a word he said. *This is different,* she told herself. *He's not Chris.* But she couldn't stop the panic from overtaking her mind.

She stared at the victim, trying to will her brain back into investigative mode. But all she could see was Chris.

"Hey, Tess. You okay?"

She tore her eyes from the victim and found Suarez giving her a questioning look.

"Um...." She could hear her pulse pound in her ears. Her heart slammed against her chest. Her throat tightened. "I'll be right back."

She turned and made her way to the front door as quickly as she could without breaking into a run. How was this happening to her? It had been almost a year since Chris's death. And she'd been doing so much better. She hadn't had an anxiety attack in months.

She kept her head down as she raced down the front steps, avoiding eye contact with the crime scene investigator she passed on her way down. Her chest tightened as she speed-walked to her car. Each breath felt harder than the last. *Just keep it together until you get to the car.* She caught the news station's van out the corner of her eye. She was relieved she'd had the foresight to park on the other end of the street.

When she reached her unmarked Ford, she threw open the driver's door. With trembling hands, she opened her purse and found the prescription bottle she'd hoped she would never need again.

After fumbling open the cap, she shook out a pill into the palm of her hand. She broke it in half before tossing the pieces into her mouth, hoping that breaking the enteric coating might help it work faster.

"You okay?" Tess heard her partner ask.

She slipped the bottle back into her purse and tossed it onto the floor of the passenger side. She heard a few pills slide out of the bottle since she hadn't closed the lid. She shuddered from the bitterness that lingered on her tongue from the broken tablet.

"I'm fine." She shut her car door and turned to face him.

Suarez held her gaze and Tess did her best to hide the physical symptoms from her internal turmoil.

"We found a suicide note signed by the son in one of the bedrooms," Suarez said after an uncomfortable silence.

"You coming back inside?"

She nodded. "I'm coming. I'll be there in just a minute."

"All right," he said before turning back toward the house.

Tess's head throbbed as she leaned against her car and took a deep breath. She jumped from the sound of her phone ringing in her pocket. She chastised herself for being so easily rattled. *Just calm down.*

She pulled out her phone but didn't recognize the

number.

"Detective Richards."

"Hi, this is Lieutenant Wallace from the Intelligence Unit. I just emailed you a formal offer letter, but I wanted to call and let you know we'd like to give you the job."

"Oh. Thank you." She wasn't expecting them to decide so soon. She'd just interviewed last Friday.

"You can let me know after you read through the offer letter, but, if you accept, we're hoping you can start as soon as possible."

She watched her partner re-enter the home and raised her hand to her temple, trying to ease the throbbing in her head brought on by the panic attack.

"I'll take the job. And I'll let you know when I can start after I talk to Lieutenant Greyson."

CHAPTER THREE

Tess was relieved when she saw Blake's unmarked Ford, identical to her own, already parked in her drive. She hadn't wanted to come home to an empty house. It was late, but she could see the lights were still on inside.

She debated whether to tell Blake about her panic attack as she got out of her car. The clonazepam had taken the edge off and allowed her to make it through the day, but she never should have taken it at work. She could have lost her job if someone had found out. You weren't supposed to even drive a car after taking that kind of drug, let alone operate a firearm.

She should've just told Suarez what was happening to her, but the attack had made her feel so...unstable. Like she wasn't cut out for the job. Didn't have what it took.

If it happened again, she'd go home. She wouldn't risk taking a drug like that at work again. She was surprised by the severity of the attack. She thought she'd dealt with her brother's death. And this was her damn job.

"Hey wifey," Blake said from the couch when she swung open the front door.

Despite the day she'd had, she couldn't help but smile

back at his handsome face. "Hi."

He moved his laptop to the side and stood as she came into the living room. His strong arms enveloped her in a hug. She noticed the weather channel played on the flatscreen on a low volume, something he always did when he worked on his cases in the evening.

She rested her head against his chest. "I still can't believe we're married."

"You better believe it." He squeezed her tighter. "Although I'm still blown away you agreed to head to Vegas last weekend. I always thought you'd want a big wedding."

"It was perfect." She had wanted the traditional wedding before Chris died, but now, she didn't want the pain of him being the only one missing from a big family affair.

"Solve your case?" he asked.

"We think so. It looks like a murder-suicide, but we have a few more people to talk to. We'll have to wait on the DNA results to make sure there was no blood present other than the father and son's. And the ME's report."

Blake took a step back and reached for her left hand. "Maybe we should tell our families this weekend about our elopement. Then we can tell work next week."

Tell work next week. She wondered how to tell Blake about the job at the Intelligence Unit. She hadn't even told him she was thinking about leaving Homicide. She hadn't wanted to seem weak.

Tess's friend from their days at the police academy had told her about the open position with the Intel Unit and encouraged her to apply. Even though she knew she needed a change, she wasn't sure she would take the job if they offered. Until today.

"Um. There's something I need to talk to you about."

His phone rang on the other side of the room. Both their heads turned toward his cell phone lying on the couch. Blake and his partner were now next up for a homicide. He crossed the room and checked his phone screen.

"It's the Chief Dispatcher." They both knew that meant he'd probably be working for the rest of the night. "That was fast," he said before answering. "Detective Stephenson."

Tess set her purse on the small accent table and sat down to take off her shoes.

"Okay. Thanks. I'll be there shortly." Blake ended the call and turned to face her. "A young woman's body was discovered in an alleyway downtown."

"I guess I'll see you tomorrow," Tess said as he moved toward her.

He bent down and kissed her softly. His lips lingered against hers, making her wish he didn't have to go.

"I love you," he said after pulling away.

"I love you, too."

She watched him grab his suit jacket off the banister before he left through the front door. She'd have to wait until tomorrow to tell him about her new job.

CHAPTER FOUR

"What do we have?"

Stephenson turned to see his shorter, more muscular partner, Detective Kyle Adams. He smelled strongly of body wash and Stephenson guessed he was at the gym when he got called to the scene.

"Patrol said it looks like a hit and run," Adams added.

Adams hopped onto a small stepladder next to Stephenson. They both stared at the victim lying in a large dumpster on top of a pile of garbage bags. The alley had been blocked off on either side. The detectives stood beneath a white, flat-top tent put in place to shield the victim from onlookers.

"Looks more like a hit, intentionally hide the body in a dumpster, and run," Adams said.

A crime scene investigator leaned into the dumpster, bagging the small pieces of trash that lay around her body. The victim was young, thin, and looked to be wearing a bit of makeup. Her short satin nightgown was stained with blood and dirt. There was no trace of any other clothing. Besides it being sleepwear, it was way too cold to be wearing such an outfit outside in Seattle in early spring.

She was barefoot, and there were tire tread marks on the lower parts of her legs and across her chest. Her skin was a mottled gray with extensive bruising beneath her clavicles.

"Who found her?" Adams asked, looking at the matted blood at the base of her scalp.

"A resident of this apartment building." Stephenson pointed to the brick structure behind the dumpster. "He was tossing his Starbucks on his way to the parking garage and caught a glimpse of her from the light from the streetlamp."

Stephenson stepped aside to give the crime scene investigator room as he turned away from the dumpster with an arm full of evidence bags.

"She's in full rigor," Stephenson added.

"You think she was killed here or somewhere else?" Adams asked.

"We found fresh skid marks and broken glass about ten feet back that way."

"So, she was probably killed sometime last night," Adams said.

"Probably. We'll see if the ME agrees."

"Does she have ID?"

Stephenson shook his head. "No. Nothing that we've found."

Adams bent over to get a closer look. He pulled a latex glove out of his pocket. "Patrol said she also had injuries across her abdomen that looked like a third set of tire marks."

"Yes."

Stephenson watched his partner carefully lift her nightgown up to her chest, exposing her underwear and the blueish-purple discoloration to her abdomen.

"CSI measured the bruising across her stomach to be about eight and a half inches wide, the same width as a standard tire, maybe a little larger."

Adams lowered her nightgown after examining her torso for a moment longer. "So, she was likely run over more than once. What is she wearing? A dress? It looks like lingerie."

"Yeah, I'm not sure."

"And no one saw it happen?" Adams asked, pulling off his glove.

"Doesn't seem that way."

Adams followed Stephenson out of the tent, and Stephenson motioned toward the adjacent building.

"The first four levels are corporate offices that operate from nine to five. Above them are residential units." Stephenson looked up the side of the old brick building. There were no balconies and it would be a hard angle to see straight down into the alley from the apartment windows. A lot of people would need to be interviewed and would probably result in nothing that would help them.

Stephenson recognized Pete, the medical examiner, walking toward them from the far end of the alley. He carried the same black bag he brought to all crime scenes.

"Good. The ME's here," Stephenson said to Adams. "Soon as he's done, let's get her out of that damn dumpster."

CHAPTER FIVE

Stephenson finished off what was left of his fourth cup of coffee before pushing the empty mug to the corner of his desk. He'd managed to go home for a few short hours of sleep after they'd done all they could the night before. Tess, at least, was sound asleep when he left.

There were no security cameras in the alleyway where the victim's body was found. Pete had estimated her time of death between midnight and four a.m. the night before her body was discovered. First thing that morning, he and Adams had interviewed more than half of the residents who overlooked the alleyway. But like he'd thought, no one had heard or seen anything out of the ordinary.

In the last hour, Pete had matched the victim's dental X-rays to a missing persons report for Andrea Morris. According to the report, Andrea was twenty-four and was last seen over two years ago.

"I just spoke with CSI," Adams said.

Stephenson turned in his seat to face his partner.

"They matched Andrea's bruising patterns to the tread of GMC stock tires found on their large SUVs and trucks after 2015."

Stephenson nodded. It was a start, but it didn't exactly narrow it down. His desk phone rang, and he picked it up after the first ring.

"Stephenson."

"Hey, it's me again."

Stephenson recognized the medical examiner's voice.

"Hey, Pete."

"I'm calling about a couple things. I've determined Andrea Morris's cause of death, and I'll be sending over my official report in a little while. She sustained more than one fatal injury, so it's hard to pinpoint which one killed her. She had displaced rib fractures which ruptured her diaphragm *and* punctured her left lung, creating a pneumothorax. *And* she sustained blunt force head trauma resulting in a subarachnoid hemorrhage."

Stephenson sighed into the phone at Pete's overuse of medical terminology. While he'd learned a lot from autopsies over his last three years as a detective, he still had to occasionally remind the ME that he was a detective, not a doctor.

"She also had a ruptured spleen," Pete continued. "Any of these could've been fatal. She incurred several non-fatal injuries as well, like a fractured pelvis and broken tibia, but I'll include all this in my report."

"So, her injuries are consistent with being run over?"

"Yes. And from the extent of her injuries, she was likely run over more than once. Possibly run over, backed over, and then run over again."

Someone wanted to make sure Andrea was dead.

"All right, thanks Pete."

"Before you go, there's one more thing I wanted to tell you. She had a brand."

"A brand?"

"Yes. You know, like the ones cattle get?"

"Yeah, I know."

"On her lower back to the left of her spine. Looks like it was done with a cauterizing pen. It's small, but it left a disfiguring scar. It looks like it could be the initials *EC*, or *CE*. It's hard to tell because the letters are kind of wrapped together in a circle. I'll attach some photos with the report. Or you're welcome to come have a look. I'll be here for the rest of the day."

"Thanks, I'd like to see it. I'll try to come by later."

"Oh—and one more thing. The label on the inside of her nightgown is Valentino."

"Okay...?"

"You know, Valentino. The designer? This nightgown probably cost something like a thousand dollars."

"Huh. All right, thanks."

Stephenson reopened Andrea's missing persons report after hanging up with the ME. Her sister had filed the report after Andrea failed to show up for their cousin's wedding. Andrea's purse and cell phone were later found in her Belltown apartment, along with seemingly all her belongings. Her car had been left parked in the parking garage. At the time the report was filed, the modeling agency Andrea worked for hadn't heard from her in two weeks.

Andrea's sister stated she'd been heavily involved in a growing self-help organization called EverChange. The organization had grown significantly in the last few years. Stephenson remembered Tess saying she had gone to a few meetings before they met, and her sister-in-law was still active in the organization. Stephenson had first heard of the Seattle-based organization through some of its high-profile members including a pitcher for the Mariners and a well-known musician.

Despite its influential supporters, the organization had been scrutinized for its exclusivity among the wealthy. It had also been criticized in the media for its rumored recruitment of young, attractive women. Just before Pete called, Stephenson had learned there was even a prominent social media hashtag protesting the organization as *#EverCult*.

"You ready?" Adams asked.

Stephenson stood from his desk and pulled on his suit jacket. "Yeah. Let's go."

It took them less than ten minutes to drive to the Pioneer Square apartment building from their downtown office. According to her missing persons report, Andrea's parents died in a car accident in 2014, leaving her sister, Savannah, her closest living relative. A small dog yapped on the other side of the door in response to Stephenson's knock.

"Georgie! Be quiet!" A woman's voice yelled from inside before the door swung open.

A tall, fit woman opened the door, holding a Yorkshire Terrier in one arm. She looked to be a few years older than her sister, probably closer to thirty. Her light brown hair was pulled into a high ponytail. The dog let out another loud bark before being shushed by its owner.

"I'm Detective Stephenson, and this is my partner, Detective Adams. Are you Savannah Morris?" Stephenson withheld the word homicide, hoping to break the news to her inside.

The woman nodded. Her expression darkened, as if knowing what they'd come to tell her. "Is this about my sister?"

"Do you mind if we come inside?"

"No, of course." She stepped aside and the detectives followed her into the apartment's small living room.

"Please have a seat." Still holding the dog, Savannah motioned toward the couch and took a seat across from them.

"We want to speak to you about your sister, Andrea," Stephenson said. "Her body was discovered late last night in an alleyway."

Savannah's lower lip quivered. "Her *body*?"

"I'm afraid so. We've matched her dental records from her missing persons report that you filed."

"Where? Here, in Seattle?"

"Yes, only a few blocks away, actually. It appears she was run over the night before last, and her body was found hidden in a dumpster. We're very sorry."

"Is there someone you can call to be with you?" Adams asked. "We can also call a chaplain to come, if you'd like?"

Savannah nodded and Adams stepped away to make the call.

Savannah wiped her tears with the back of her hand. "So, it wasn't an accident?"

"We're not sure," Stephenson said. "At the very least, whoever hit her attempted to hide her body before fleeing the scene. But we believe she may've been hit intentionally, yes."

"I was afraid something like this would happen. She was so involved in that cult. They brainwashed her. Then, when she went missing..." her voice broke, and she looked away from the detective.

Stephenson waited in silence for her to continue. She

cleared her throat.

"There have been a lot of times in the last two years I thought she was already dead."

"And why is that?" Stephenson asked as Adams stepped back into the room.

"Because of EverChange. There was creepy stuff going on inside that cult. They front themselves as an elite self-help organization and target wealthy, attractive, and influential people. Then, they use those members to recruit more like them. People seem to not question it because of some of the celebrities that are involved."

Stephenson could think of a few, including a Seattle-born singer who had won a nationally-televised, prime-time talent show a few years back. From his quick research at the Homicide Unit, EverChange was only in Seattle, but had plans to expand to L.A. in the next year.

"It seemed okay at first. Andrea was so excited about it." Savannah rolled her eyes. "Then, she started pulling away from all her friends that weren't in EverChange. Even me. She turned down modeling jobs, which had been her dream, to attend these ridiculous EverChange seminars. She was spending all her money on them. Even took out a loan to pay for this 'exclusive training' they were offering. It was really sad watching her give up her life for them. She tried to get me to join, and, when I wouldn't, it got hard for me to get a hold of her. Before that though...she told me some really weird stuff."

"Like what?" Stephenson asked.

"Like that EverChange was teaching her leadership through servitude and someone in the organization was her *master*, and she had to do anything and everything they said. She had to have her phone on twenty-four hours a day, and she'd even go run an errand for them in the middle of the night. Who knows what all they were making her do. I told her it was nuts, but she said I just didn't understand.

"She went on and on about how EverChange had helped her heal from our painful childhood. And how I was creating my own limitations by choosing not to become enlightened. She even said she felt sorry for me when I refused to 'evolve'. Eventually, she stopped talking to me.

"After she missed our cousin's wedding, I called the modeling agency she worked for and found out she'd quit. She'd wanted to be a model since we were little kids. It didn't make any sense. I knew something was wrong. That's when I went to her apartment and found her car and all her stuff. But not Andrea."

"Did you contact EverChange to find out if they knew where she was?" Adams asked.

"Yeah. I knew from Andrea that they meet in people's homes or high-end venues. So, I called the number listed online. At first, they wouldn't give me any information because I'm not a member. I finally found a listed address, an office on Capitol Hill. When I told the woman working there that I'd filed a missing persons report on Andrea, she told me Andrea hadn't been to a meeting in over a month, but they would ask her to call me the next time she came." Savannah shook her head. "Which, of course, she never did."

Savannah looked out her living room window as fresh tears streamed down her face. "I drove by that office the other day but now it's a coffee shop. You said she was found a few blocks from here? Where has she been all this time?"

"If we find out, we'll let you know," Stephenson said.

After the chaplain arrived, Stephenson stood and

handed Savannah his card. "We're very sorry for your loss. If you think of anything else that might help us, please let me know. We'll see ourselves out."

She nodded and accepted the card. The chaplain looked probably close to fifty. His kind eyes focused on Savannah as he took a seat across from her. Pulling her dog closer, she stared out her living room window as the detectives left her apartment.

"Looks like we need to do some checking into EverChange," Adams said when they got back to their car.

"Yes, it does." Stephenson didn't know much about the organization, but he didn't disagree with Andrea's sister that it sounded like a cult. All that he knew about the group was that the founder was Colton Everett, a well-known Seattle financier and real estate developer who'd revamped several Seattle neighborhoods and industrial areas. Everett had been in the national news a few years back when his wife had fallen to her death when the couple was hiking Mount Rainier.

"I'll track down Colton Everett. I think we need to interview him face-to-face. You want to see what you can find on the organization?"

"Sounds good," Adams said.

When they got back to the Homicide Unit, Stephenson was surprised to see Tess sitting in Greyson's office. They looked to be having a serious conversation. At first, he wondered if she might be informing him of their recent marriage, but he didn't think she would do that without him. He tried not to stare as he passed by the glass windows of the lieutenant's office on his way to his desk.

It didn't take him long to find an address for Colton Everett.

Stephenson spun in his chair to face his partner. "I've got an address for Colton Everett. A condo in a luxury downtown high-rise close to the waterfront. You want to come with me to interview him?"

"Sure," Adams said, his eyes still focused on his computer screen. "Check this out." He tilted his screen toward Stephenson's desk. "Savannah was right. The Capitol Hill EverChange office no longer exists. But EverChange owns this massive estate on the bluffs of Whidbey Island. It was built in 1908. This is a *non-profit* organization and they bought it three years ago for over ten million."

Stephenson raised his eyebrows at the large stone mansion. It looked more like a castle than a home. Tall evergreens lined the landscaped property on either side. From the aerial photo, the grounds included a pool, helicopter pad, and small private airstrip.

"According to Zillow," Adams said, "the house is twenty thousand square feet."

"I wonder what a non-profit organization is using a place like that for."

"Wellness retreats?" Adams grinned. "I think I'd be feeling pretty good after spending some time at a place like that."

Adams flicked off his screen and followed Stephenson out of the unit. Tess stood from her chair when they reached the lieutenant's office. Stephenson slowed as the office door opened, curious as to what she was speaking to their superior about.

"We'll be sorry to see you go," Stephenson heard the

lieutenant say as Tess came out of his office.

Her eyes widened when she saw her husband standing outside the doorway. She turned back to the lieutenant. "Thank you," she said before closing the door.

"Sorry to see you go where?" Stephenson asked as she stepped into the hall.

Tess glanced uncomfortably at Adams.

"Looks like I'll see you in the car," he said to Stephenson.

"I wanted to tell you last night, but I didn't get the chance," Tess said when they were alone in the hall. "I've taken a job with the Intelligence Unit."

"What? When?"

"They offered me the job yesterday."

"Without even interviewing?"

"Well, no. I interviewed last Friday."

"And you didn't think to tell me?"

"I—I did. I just didn't plan on taking the job."

"Then why'd you interview?"

Out the corner of her eye, Tess caught Greyson staring at them from behind his desk.

"Can we talk about this later? At home?"

Stephenson couldn't understand why she'd kept this from him. Especially now that they were married. *Weren't married people supposed to tell each other everything? Or, at least, major life decisions?*

"Fine."

She gave him an apologetic look before he turned in the opposite direction.

Stephenson recognized the Pearl Jam song Adams was listening to as he approached the passenger door of his partner's unmarked Ford. Adams turned down the volume as Stephenson climbed inside.

"Trouble in paradise?" Adams asked.

Stephenson reached behind his shoulder for his seat belt. "Let's go."

CHAPTER SIX

Adams pulled to a stop in front of the gated entrance to Colton Everett's Whidbey Island estate. Tall evergreens surrounded the property and the detectives were unable to see the mansion from where they were parked.

When they had gone to Colton Everett's downtown apartment, there had been no answer. They'd learned from the front desk that they hadn't seen him in two weeks. They checked the parking garage and his designated parking spot was empty.

"If Andrea came all the way from this estate on the night she was killed, why wasn't she wearing more clothes?" Adams asked.

"What is that?" Stephenson pointed to a tall structure beyond the gate. It looked like a treehouse. "Some sort of lookout tower?"

Adams rolled down his window and was about to press the intercom when a petite dark-haired woman climbed down the built-in steps of the small wooden structure with an AR-15 style rifle slung over her shoulder. She wore ripped jeans and a fitted sweater. Her rifle swayed behind her shoulder as she moved toward the gate.

Adams and Stephenson stepped out of the car as she approached.

"Can I help you?" she asked.

"I'm Detective Adams from the Seattle Police, Homicide Unit. This is my partner, Detective Stephenson. We're here to speak with Colton Everett."

She looked back and forth between the detectives through her aviator sunglasses. "Sorry," she finally said. "He's not here."

"Do you know when he might be back?" Stephenson asked. "We're happy to come in and wait."

She shook her head. "I'm afraid I don't know when he'll be back. And we don't allow uninvited visitors on the property. I mean, unless you have a warrant?"

"Are you employed here? As security?" Adams asked.

She let out a short laugh. "Work here? No. I'm just protecting our property. And I know I'm well within my rights. I'll let Colton know you came by. But, like I said, I have no idea when he'll be back."

"Do you know where he is?" Stephenson asked.

"Sorry, I don't."

But she didn't look sorry at all.

Adams passed his card through the gate. "Have him give me a call when he gets back."

She hesitated before accepting the card. The detectives watched her return to her station in the lookout tower as Adams pulled away from the drive.

"That was bizarre," Stephenson said. "Why would they need an armed guard at their front gate? Makes me wonder what they're hiding."

"Yeah. And too bad she's a part of that weird organization."

"Why's that?"

Adams grinned. "I kinda liked her."

Stephenson shook his head and looked out his window at the tall evergreens that lined the windy road. *Some things never change.*

Stephenson sipped his fifth coffee of the day as he zoomed in on the gated compound on the satellite image on his laptop. He'd switched to decaf in the hope of getting some sleep tonight. On their way back from Whidbey Island, Stephenson had found Colton's cell number in their Accurint database and left a voicemail. But he still hadn't returned his call.

Colton had two cars registered in his name, a new Maserati and a 1962 Ferrari 250 GTO, neither of which could've been what ran Andrea over. Although he knew Everett was rich, he was surprised to see that he owned that particular model of Ferrari. He'd recently read online that one had sold at auction for nearly fifty million dollars.

When Stephenson searched for cars registered to EverChange, he'd found what he was looking for. There were six GMC SUVs registered to the non-profit, and all of them would have tires that matched the tread patterns found on Andrea's body.

On his way home from the Homicide Unit, he'd picked up a thumb drive from the Seattle Department of Transportation office with the footage from downtown traffic cameras on the night of Andrea's murder. There were also several red light cameras downtown, but Washington State law barred him from being able to access or use their images for anything other than a traffic violation. He'd been looking at the footage for the last hour and hadn't found any of the SUVs belonging to EverChange or any vehicles with the damage he'd expect after running over the victim.

Stephenson leaned back against the leather couch and glanced at his front door. The sun had set a couple of hours earlier. He expected Tess home any minute.

His eyes needed a break from all the traffic cam footage, and Stephenson refocused his attention on the satellite image of the EverChange compound on Whidbey Island. Stephenson knew Everett had money, but this estate must've cost a fortune. And the tree-lined, gated perimeter dotted with security lookouts was too over-the-top for just protecting a private residence, even one as expensive as this.

A mansion that looked more like a castle stood in the middle of the twenty-five-acre property. The grounds were immaculately landscaped. A long, circular driveway led to the estate. There was a large sculpted fountain in the center of it at the entrance to the home. Beyond the mansion's lawn were bluffs that dropped off to the Puget Sound. The mansion would have views of Mount Baker protruding from the North Cascades in the distance.

Stephenson opened a new window and did an Internet search of the property's address. He found the real estate listing from three years earlier when the estate had been on the market for nearly ten million. It was built in 1905 by a prominent financier, born in New York and eventually settling in the Pacific Northwest, who'd invested heavily in railroads. And, the reason the home looked like a castle...was because it was. The original owner had a Welsh castle dismantled and then shipped the deconstructed parts to Puget Sound to be used for the estate's building materials. The home's exterior and much of its interior were over five hundred years old, making it the oldest and only Tudor-Gothic castle of its kind in the United States.

Stephenson had lived his whole life in the Seattle area but had never heard of this place.

He reopened the traffic cam footage and started with the camera closest to where Andrea was found. Over an hour later, he rubbed his eyes.

He wouldn't be able to get through all the footage that night. But he hoped that if they could find an EverChange SUV on a downtown traffic camera, he could get a judge to approve a warrant for the vehicle and maybe even the Whidbey Island estate.

He was about to close his laptop, thinking it would be best if he started fresh early in the morning. But there was one more thing he wanted to know.

He opened a new browser window and searched for *Colton Everett wife.* Stephenson clicked on the headline at the top of the search results: *WIFE OF BILLIONAIRE REAL ESTATE DEVELOPER DEATH RULED AN ACCIDENT.*

The news article loaded just as Tess came in through the front door.

CHAPTER SEVEN

Blake set aside his laptop when Tess came inside. She could tell he was tired but was unable to read any more than that from his expression. She set her purse on the entry way table before taking a seat next to him on the couch.

"I'm sorry I didn't tell you earlier about the job."

"I can't believe you didn't even tell me you interviewed for it. I thought we were closer than that. I mean, we're *married*."

She didn't know what to say. She hadn't meant to keep it from him, but for some reason, she had.

"Why didn't you tell me?"

She looked into his eyes and they told her he wasn't angry. Just hurt.

"I didn't know you wanted to work for the Intel Unit," he said. "You've always said you wanted to be a homicide detective since you were a teenager."

Despite their being together less than two years, he knew her better than anyone else.

"I never planned on taking it. I wasn't looking to apply for another job, but my friend from the academy told me the Intel Unit had a position open and encouraged me to apply. At first, I told her I wasn't interested. But there are times when I'm working my homicide cases I feel constantly reminded of Chris's death. So, I figured there was no harm in applying and learning a little more about the job. I didn't expect them to offer it to me."

"I still don't get why you didn't say anything to me. And I would've thought you could've mentioned it at least before you gave your notice to Greyson."

"I hadn't planned on telling him today. The Intel Unit only offered me the job yesterday, but they called today and said they had an assignment they want me to take and asked if I can start tomorrow."

"*Tomorrow?* What's the assignment?"

"I don't know. They want me to go undercover this weekend, and they're going to prep me tomorrow."

He raised his eyebrows. "Undercover? You think you're ready for that? And you don't even know what you're going undercover *for?*"

She tried not to be offended that he might not think she could handle it, hoping his skepticism was only out of concern. She thought about telling him about her anxiety attack yesterday but decided against it. It was out of the blue, and she didn't want him to think she was...unstable.

"I've been having a hard time with Chris's death lately. Especially at work."

He took her hand. "I know."

She was surprised to feel tears come to her eyes.

"But are you sure you should be jumping into an undercover assignment when you're having a hard time at work?"

She felt her body tense. "Just because certain murder scenes trigger my memories of Chris's death doesn't mean

I'm not fit to go undercover. Yes, I'm having trouble dealing with my emotions with murder investigations. But I'm still capable of doing something just as important, like going undercover with Intelligence."

"You know I will always support you, and you can tell me anything."

His words made her feel horrible for keeping it from him.

"But, moving forward, I need to know that you're not keeping things like this from me. Secrets."

"I know. I should've told you. I'm sorry."

"I just need to know the real you."

She nodded. "Okay." Although, lately, she wasn't sure she knew who the *real her* was.

CHAPTER EIGHT

Stephenson turned into the courthouse parking garage the next morning just as his phone rang. He was surprised to see Adams calling him that early.

"Morning sunshine," Stephenson said.

"Hey, are you on your way in?" Adams asked.

"I'm actually at the courthouse. Did you see my text?"

"Yeah I got the text. That's why I'm calling—"

"I found an SUV belonging to EverChange on our traffic cam footage." Stephenson got out of his car. "There was no damage to the vehicle and you can't see the driver, but it could've been before they ran her over. Anyway, I asked Judge Tanner if I could see her before she goes to court this morning. I'm going to see if she'll grant us a warrant for the vehicle and the Whidbey Island property."

"Blake, Lieutenant Greyson wants to meet with us. Before you ask Judge Tanner for that warrant."

"What? Why? I can't. If I don't see her now, she won't be available again until tonight. Did you tell him this is a *murder* investigation? We can't risk giving EverChange more time to get rid of the evidence on the vehicle I identified."

"I know. I told him. But he says he needs to speak with

us before you get that warrant. There's a bunch of big wigs waiting for us in the conference room. Including the Chief of Police. It's about EverChange, but they won't tell me what's going on until you get here, too."

Stephenson paused at the door to the courthouse before turning around. "Fine. I think this is a mistake, but I'm on my way. This better be good."

Adams met Stephenson in the hall of the Homicide Unit and Stephenson followed him to their conference room. The room had windows on two sides, offering views of the Seattle waterfront. As surprised as he'd been to hear the Police Chief wanted to see them, he was even more taken aback by the number of people seated around the conference table. The Chief of Police sat at one end next to Amber, a detective from the Sex Crimes Unit who'd recently transferred to the High Risk Victims Unit. A lieutenant from the Intelligence Unit sat to their left, along with Stephenson's stickler superior, Lieutenant Greyson, and several other people he didn't recognize. Stephenson took a seat next to his partner at the last open seat at the table.

The Chief of Police cleared his throat. "Great. Now that we're all here," he said, eyeing Stephenson and Adams, "we can get started."

Now that we're all here? Stephenson thought. It wasn't even eight o' clock, and he hadn't gotten any emails about a meeting this morning. And why were he and Adams the only homicide detectives in the room?

"It's come to our attention that you, Detective Stephenson, believe your recent homicide case is connected to Colton Everett, the founder of EverChange. *And* that you plan to request a search warrant of his Whidbey Island residence after you and Detective Adams visited the property asking to speak with him."

Stephenson glanced at his partner. "Yes, that's correct. I also found an SUV registered to EverChange on a downtown traffic camera the night Andrea Morris was killed. CSI has matched that vehicle's standard tire specs, including the tread, to the bruising pattern found on the victim's body."

The Chief folded his hands atop the table. "I'm requesting that you wait on that search warrant, as it would interfere with several ongoing investigations into both Everett and his organization, EverChange."

"*What?* What about *our* investigation? A woman has been killed. If we don't search that property, or that vehicle soon, evidence could be destroyed."

The Chief looked unmoved by what Stephenson had said. "Colton Everett and his organization, EverChange, are currently under investigation by the IRS for tax evasion, the FBI for racketeering, and Seattle's High Risk Victim's Unit for human trafficking. The Intelligence Unit has been liaising information among these three agencies throughout the investigations."

Stephenson opened his mouth to speak but the Chief continued.

"Some of these investigations have been ongoing for over a year, and we cannot allow you to impede them by searching his Whidbey Island premises or pressuring him to speak to you about your recent homicide. And, for reasons I cannot disclose, our state governor has a personal interest in these EverChange investigations."

Stephenson tried to contain a look of shock.

"So, until you have substantial evidence linking Everett to your homicide investigation, we're suggesting you turn your efforts in another direction. We are very close to arresting him on several charges. Once we do, you'll be welcome to interview him. *And* search the Whidbey Island compound if you can prove just cause."

Stephenson looked at Adams in disbelief, then back to the Chief.

"So, you want to jeopardize our *homicide* investigation because EverChange is under investigation by the IRS? You want us to look the other way so you can arrest him on *tax evasion* and *racketeering*? And the gov—"

"There's more at stake here than the death of one person." The Chief nodded to Amber on his right. She locked eyes with Stephenson before speaking.

"A year ago, a woman filed a police report accusing Colton Everett of recruiting women into EverChange for the purpose of sex trafficking. She stated that Everett used forms of blackmail and coercion to impose forced sex and embezzlement of women at his Whidbey Island estate after he lured them into the organization through promises of self-help, prestige, and exclusivity. Everett's attorneys denied these claims before posting videos of this woman trash-talking her family and close friends for being unsupportive of her involvement in EverChange. After the videos were posted, she retracted all her statements and dropped the charges against EverChange, claiming that she'd made it all up.

"Six months ago, another woman came forward, Taylor Neilson. She filed a report with similar claims. That she'd been recruited by Everett to join the elite self-help world of EverChange. She stated that Everett gradually sucked her into his world of coercion, masking his lies and manipulation as allegiance to the group. In the report, she also said she was later forced to perform sex acts for Everett as dictated by him being her 'master' in the organization. But—"

"So why didn't you search Everett's compound on Whidbey Island then? And why should we wait? Our homicide victim could be proof that his violence against these women is progressing, which needs to be stopped."

"I don't disagree," Amber said. "Taylor committed suicide the day after she filed the report. She overdosed on a bottle of Xanax she'd been prescribed to treat anxiety at her parents' weekend home on Vashon Island. Colton Everett was questioned with his attorneys present about her death and her claims. He was cooperative but denied everything. Her police report didn't specify where all the sex crimes had taken place, but I was granted a search warrant for his downtown apartment. However, the search turned up nothing. I was hoping to at least find a laptop or some sort of personal device that we could extract information from, but there wasn't anything. We now believe he keeps everything at his Whidbey compound. After my search of his downtown residence yielded nothing, I couldn't get the judge to approve another warrant for his Whidbey Island property."

"Are you sure her death was a suicide?" Adams asked.

Amber nodded. "Yes. Her death was thoroughly investigated by King County Major Crimes. There was no evidence of anything other than suicide."

Adams and Stephenson exchanged a look that they both knew meant, *We'll look into that.*

"I still don't see why we can't search his property,

especially now that Everett is connected to a homicide," Stephenson said.

Amber turned to the Intelligence Unit lead. "Lieutenant Wallace?"

The lieutenant cleared her throat. "We're unsure at this point about the level of criminal activity taking place within EverChange. Because Everett's Whidbey Island estate is owned by EverChange, a non-profit organization, it's more difficult to justify a search warrant." Wallace pursed her lips before continuing. "If we searched the property today, we may never be able to prove the extent of criminal activity going on within this organization. If the women are coerced and staying at the property out of a perceived allegiance to EverChange, they might not admit to the abuse they've sustained. Our best chances are to send someone in undercover, a woman, who can later testify to what's really going on behind those walls. We have a plan to send someone in tonight, if everything goes smoothly. We should be able to arrest Everett within a month. And make it an arrest that will ensure his conviction and a life behind bars."

Stephenson was speechless. He thought immediately of Tess. The timing of her transferring to the Intelligence Unit. *Could she be the woman they were sending undercover? Would they send her into something like that so soon?* But he didn't dare ask. Not here. Not now.

Stephenson shook his head in frustration before standing from his seat. With his partner still seated at the table, he walked out of the conference room without another word.

CHAPTER NINE

The Intelligence Unit lieutenant stood next to the large screen in the windowless conference room. Tess stared at the photo of Colton Everett, who smiled between the founder of a Seattle-based tech company and the Washington State Governor. His wavy brown hair and pronounced jaw had always reminded her of JFK Jr. She was surprised at the butterflies that formed in her stomach after seeing his picture.

"Colton Everett, billionaire real estate developer, financier, and the founder of EverChange, is the focus of your investigation. He's under investigation for tax evasion, racketeering, and sex trafficking." Lieutenant Wallace shifted her gaze from the screen and locked eyes with Tess. "As you know, he has a thing for tall, beautiful blondes under thirty. Given your history, he should approach you tonight at the meeting. If he doesn't, we want you to approach him."

Tess wouldn't exactly say she and Colton had *history*. They only went on one date. It was right before she became a homicide detective. Their date had gone well. They definitely had chemistry. But she got the feeling Colton hadn't liked the fact she was a cop. He'd recently broken up with his girlfriend, Avery, whom he got back together with shortly after he and Tess had gone out.

When she got the job with homicide, she stopped going to the EverChange meetings. They had started to feel a little hokey, and she didn't want to deal with the awkwardness of seeing Colton after their one-off date.

Tess shifted in her seat, fighting the rising anxiety in her chest. She wasn't expecting to go undercover so soon. She figured she'd have more time to mentally prepare.

After she'd arrived at the Intelligence Unit offices that morning, she had been briefed on her assignment: go undercover in the EverChange organization at their compound on Whidbey Island. The Intelligence Unit was already aware of Tess's history with EverChange and her sister-in-law's current involvement, which they planned on using to get Tess inside the organization.

Tess realized that she hadn't chosen to join the Intel Unit. They'd recruited *her*. They opened the position and had her friend from the academy encourage her to apply because of her connection to Colton Everett.

Wallace clicked to the next photo of a young, pretty brunette. She smiled broadly and looked to be about twenty years old.

"This is Charity Green. The governor's daughter. We believe she's at the compound but are unsure of her wellbeing. If and when you get to the compound, we need you to find out if she's there and get her out safely before we raid the place, if that's what it comes down to."

Before Tess had time to respond, the lieutenant brought up another photo. Tess recognized the woman in the photograph with Colton. Avery Hill. The Seattle-born singer had recently won a nationally televised, prime-time talent show. She'd also made the headlines for her romantic involvement with EverChange's wealthy founder. Like Tess, Avery was tall, with full lips and long blonde hair. They looked like they could be sisters.

"Avery Hill, Colton's fiancé, might be at the meeting tonight, as well. We want you to also connect with her. Getting Avery and Colton to believe you're searching for something to help you heal from your brother's death is our best chance of you getting invited to the Whidbey estate."

A new photo filled the screen. A dark-haired man smiled next to Colton. They both wore suits. Tess realized who the man was before Wallace spoke.

"Antonio Ramirez, pitcher for the Mariners, is one of several local celebrities you might bump into tonight." She clicked to the next screen and brought up another photo of Colton and an older man Tess instantly recognized. The Grammy-winning musician had his arm around Colton. They looked like they were on the back of a yacht. "Another is singer-songwriter, Alexander Hall." Wallace clicked to the next screen, a blown-up image of the cover of *Forbes*. A young woman with a sleek black bob graced the cover, smiling with her arms crossed. There was a bold headline next to her photo: *WEALTHIEST CEOS UNDER 30*

Lieutenant Wallace turned to face Tess. "Rachelle Morales, co-founder and CEO of Datix, a Seattle-based tech company, has also been recently connected with EverChange."

Tess watched Wallace's expression change as a new image filled the screen. A young woman, wearing a dirt and blood-stained nightgown, lay in a dumpster among loose trash and garbage bags. Tess could tell she was deceased from her severely bruised and mottled, pale-gray skin.

Wallace looked at the photo as she spoke. "This is the body of twenty-four-year-old Andrea Morris. She was found the night before last in a downtown alley. She'd been run over, probably more than once, before her body was thrown into a dumpster."

Blake's new homicide case.

The lieutenant cleared her throat before she continued. "Her friends and family last saw her two years ago, and we believe she'd been staying at the EverChange compound on Whidbey Island prior to her death. CSI has matched the tread pattern on her bruising to the stock tires placed on newer models of GMC SUVs and trucks, and EverChange has six of these vehicles registered under the non-profit."

Wallace brought up another photograph and it took Tess a moment to tell what she was looking at.

"This is a postmortem photo of a brand found on Andrea Morris's lower back. We believe the women at the EverChange compound are being branded somehow with the overlapping letters, *EC*. Either for EverChange...or Colton Everett."

Tess examined the photo until Wallace turned off the screen. She'd never seen anything like that on a human being.

"Any questions?" Wallace asked.

An overwhelming doubt loomed in Tess's mind. "They know I'm a detective. Even if they didn't already, in the articles about Chris's death, I've been listed as a homicide detective. And my face has been in the news in connection with other cases. Won't they be leery of inviting a detective to their compound where they're engaging in criminal activity?"

"Not necessarily. Colton is arrogant, and we believe he thrives on getting celebrities and public figures to join his organization. In addition to the media attention they provide, he uses celebrities to provide legitimacy to his cult. He seems to think they provide a shield against public criticism, and to an extent, they do.

"We're hoping he'll feel the same about a detective. But we think your chances of acceptance will be higher if you're an *ex* member of law enforcement. Which is why, as of today, you are no longer a detective. At least, not officially. We'll be sending a press release to all the major media channels later today. It will state that you've resigned from the police department for personal reasons. With all the media attention surrounding your brother's death and murder trial, and your older brother being a well-known Seahawk player, we're confident the story will get ample coverage. This is your cover, and it's what you will tell any friends and family who ask."

Tess pressed her lips together and stared at the photo of Colton on the wall.

"You'll tell your sister-in-law before the meeting tonight that you quit because the job was a constant reminder of Chris's death, and you lost your confidence in the justice system after what happened at his trial. And that you're hoping EverChange can help redirect you both personally and professionally."

After what happened at his trial. Tess tried to hide her emotions from the painful reminder that her brother's killer had yet to, and might never, be brought to justice for murdering Chris.

"The story will break at four p.m., and we want you to be out of the office before that," Wallace continued. "Have you heard back from your sister-in-law?"

Tess nodded. "She confirmed there's a meeting tonight and that she would take me with her."

"Good. We need Everett to believe you are desperate for an escape from the press and from the upcoming re-trial of your brother's murder. You'll have to convince him of this at the meeting tonight. That you can't stand to go home, and you're looking to EverChange to provide solace for you during this time."

Tess felt guilty knowing she wouldn't be present at the re-trial of Chris's murder. She'd used up all her time off to be present at the first trial, which resulted in a hung jury. She still couldn't believe it. The evidence against her brother's killer was overwhelming. But part of her was glad she wouldn't have to sit through the gut-wrenching experience again. She didn't think she could bear it if they didn't get a conviction this time.

"We need you to get inside the Whidbey Island compound. We don't expect him to invite you there after only one meeting, but we want you to try. So, say whatever you need to so that he invites you there tonight."

"And what if he doesn't?"

"Then you'll have to wait until there's another meeting and try again. If you *do* get taken to the compound tonight, we wouldn't expect Colton to allow you to see any of the criminal activity that's going on until he believes you've been indoctrinated enough to go along with it. So, the sooner you earn his trust by convincing him of your allegiance to EverChange, the better. *And*, we expect they'll ask you to give up your phone."

"But how will I communicate what's going on back to the department?"

"We don't want to risk your cover by sending you in with a wire or any sort of listening device. But we have an exit plan for you already in place. EverChange employs a local landscape company to work on the grounds every Friday. There will be another intelligence unit detective working undercover as one of the landscapers. He'll be wearing a red 49ers hat. He'll be waiting for a signal from you each week, so you'll have to be sure to make contact with him.

"He's going to ask you, *Having a good day, ma'am?* If you need out, you'll say no. If you're safe to stay, you'll say yes. We're planning a raid on the compound exactly three weeks after you arrive, unless you need out before then."

"What do I tell my hu-boyfriend?" They hadn't been married when she'd interviewed for the job. She knew she should say that he was now her husband, but it didn't feel right telling her new boss, someone she barely knew, before she told her family.

"That you're going to an EverChange meeting with your sister-in-law. Nothing more."

CHAPTER TEN

Stephenson checked his email when he got to his desk after the frustrating meeting. While he scanned his inbox, he pressed his cell phone to his ear, hoping he could catch Tess before she started her workday. But her phone went straight to voicemail. He hung up without leaving a message.

He forced the idea that Tess was the one that Intel was planning to send undercover into the EverChange mansion out of his mind. He told himself there were several reasons why that couldn't be.

He was glad to see he'd received the autopsy and police report for Everett's late wife done four years prior. Stephenson decided to read through the Pierce County Medical Examiner's report first. It would at least distract him from worrying about Tess.

Parker Everett had fallen over one hundred feet to her death from Barrier Peak, a popular summit over 6,000 feet in elevation. The medical examiner determined her death to have resulted from multiple severe injuries sustained from her fall, including a brain hemorrhage and broken neck. There was no physical evidence pointing to her fall being anything but accidental. According to her husband, Colton

Everett, Parker had been posing for a photo before she slipped and fell backward over the summit's steep edge. She was twenty-eight years old.

Stephenson went through the police case file next. Parker and Colton had been married for less than three years when she died. She'd had no life insurance policy, and, with Colton's net worth of over a billion dollars, money didn't seem to be a motive.

The detectives' interviews of Parker's and Colton's friends and family didn't turn up anything significant. They confirmed that both Colton and Parker had been avid hikers. Some stated the couple had fights on and off, but they always resulted in making up. Stephenson noted Colton founded EverChange only six months after Parker's death.

After he finished reading the report, he pulled up a news article about Parker's death. A photo of Colton and Parker topped the article, both smiling with their arms wrapped around each other. Stephenson could tell from the photo Parker had been very beautiful. Like Tess, she was tall, with long blonde hair and blue eyes. The article stated Parker was a former model and enjoyed hiking in the Pacific Northwest since she was a little girl. There was another photo of Parker as an eight-year-old girl, smiling with her parents and older brother on a hike in the Olympic Mountains.

Stephenson closed out of the article and re-opened the police report. At the time of the report, Parker's parents lived in Sequim, a quaint seaside town two hours northwest of Seattle. He dialed the number listed in the report for Parker's father. He answered on the second ring.

"Hello?"

"Hi. Is this Curtis Redding?"

"Yes."

"This is Detective Stephenson from the Seattle Homicide Unit. Colton Everett has come up in connection with a recent investigation, and I was wondering if I could speak with you and your wife about Colton and his relationship to your late daughter, Parker?"

"My wife passed away over a year ago. Ovarian cancer."

"Oh, I'm very sorry to hear that."

"Thank you. But, yes, I'd be happy to answer your questions. You said you're from Homicide? Is Colton a murder suspect?"

"At this point, I'm just seeking more information about him, and I'd like to ask some questions about his marriage to your daughter. Are you still living in Sequim? I'd like to speak to you in person, if possible. I can come to you."

The conversation could be done over the phone, but Stephenson wanted to look Parker's father in the eyes when he asked him about Colton.

"Yes, I am. But I'm visiting my son in Victoria until tomorrow. I'll be taking the ferry back to Port Angeles in the morning. Should be home by one."

"Great. I'll stop by tomorrow afternoon. You're still at the same address?"

"Yes. Same one for thirty years now."

"Okay, I'll see you then. Thank you."

After hanging up, Stephenson went back through the case file on Parker's death. Something seemed to be missing. Or perhaps overlooked. He lifted his desk phone and dialed the number for the Pierce County homicide detective listed as the lead investigator.

"Detective Samuels," an older woman's voice came though the line.

"Hi, this is Detective Stephenson from Seattle

Homicide. I'm calling regarding the death of Parker Everett. Her surviving husband has come up in connection to a recent homicide, and I received her case file from your records department this morning. You were listed as the lead investigator four years ago."

"Yes. I remember that case well."

"I noticed there was no mention in her file whether she and her husband, Colton Everett, had a prenup. Do you remember if they did?"

"As far as I'm aware, there wasn't, but I'm not 100 percent sure. It's not in the file?"

"No. There's no mention of whether they had one or not."

"Well, there was no evidence suggesting anything other than an accidental fall. And we confirmed there was no life insurance policy on her. And, with Everett's bank account, we were able to rule out money as a motive. If I remember correctly, they'd been married only about three years and, as far as we could prove, they were happy. I don't remember any specifics about a prenup, but, whether they did or didn't, wouldn't have changed the determination of my investigation."

"All right. Thanks for your time."

"Sure. What's Colton Everett connected with this time?"

"A young woman's body was found in a downtown alley the night before last. She'd been run over and then her body hidden in a dumpster. She was a member of EverChange, Everett's non-profit organization."

"Hmm. Well, good luck with *that*. You guys get all the hot-shot cases up there. Don't envy you on this one, though."

Stephenson was aware of Adams returning to his desk

while he was on the phone, but his focus was fixed on his computer screen after hanging up. He ran an Internet search of *Colton Everett 2017*. He found the article he was looking for near the top of the results. He remembered it coming up when he'd searched Colton's name the night before. *COLTON EVERETT SEEN WITH NEW LOVE INTEREST ONLY A MONTH AFTER WIFE'S TRAGIC DEATH*. He clicked on the article.

A slightly grainy image loaded beneath the headline of Colton holding hands with a tall blonde outside a restaurant on Whidbey Island. They both wore sunglasses, and the woman bore a striking resemblance to Parker. The photo was dated a day after Pierce County detectives ruled Parker's fall accidental.

"I'm gonna get some coffee," he heard Adams say. "You want some?"

"Sure." Stephenson handed him his empty coffee mug without taking his eyes from his screen. He zoomed in on the photo as Adams stepped out of their cubicle. *If they didn't have a prenup, Parker could've gotten half of Colton's fortune in a divorce. Seems like he had a motive for murder after all.*

Stephenson stood from his chair at ten minutes to four. If he wanted to catch Lieutenant Greyson before he left for the day, Stephenson didn't have much time. His superior never stayed a minute past his eight-hour workday.

Tess had never returned his call, but he figured she was busy with her first day at the Intel Unit. The more he'd thought about it throughout the day, it seemed crazy to think she'd be the one they were sending undercover at the EverChange mansion. The Intel Unit had obviously been planning the undercover mission for a while, and Tess had barely set foot in the department.

Stephenson found Greyson sitting behind his oversized desk, running his palm atop the back of thinning hair. He looked less than thrilled when Stephenson entered his office.

"Detective, I was just about to leave for the day."

Stephenson took a seat across from him. "This won't take long."

The lieutenant frowned. "I hope not."

"What did the Chief mean when he said that the governor had a special interest in EverChange? Like, she's a member or what?"

Greyson leaned forward and folded his hands atop his desk. "I know you're not used to having information withheld from you, but I'm afraid I'm not at liberty to say."

The lieutenant's frown had disappeared suddenly and Stephenson thought he looked like he was enjoying this.

"It just doesn't make any sense to me why her *interest* in EverChange should have anything to do with how the organization is being investigated. Or my homicide case, for that matter."

Greyson shifted in his seat. "I wouldn't say her interest is impacting *how* EverChange is being investigated. And it's more of a *personal* interest that requires tact and, in this case, confidentiality. If I could tell you, believe me, I would."

Stephenson wasn't so sure.

The lieutenant uncrossed his hands. "Is there anything else?"

Stephenson stood from his chair. He wanted to ask about who the Intel Unit was planning to send undercover into EverChange, but he couldn't. Even though they hadn't told the department about their marriage, it was no secret that he and Tess were a couple. And Stephenson wasn't sure if Greyson knew she'd taken on a job at the Intel Unit.

"No. Thanks." *For nothing.*

CHAPTER ELEVEN

Tess pressed her lips together as she replaced the cap on her lipstick. She eyed herself in her bathroom mirror and ran her hand through her long blonde hair. She'd applied way more makeup than what she usually wore, but she needed Colton to notice her for something other than being a detective.

Her heart began to race as she thought about her assignment. She didn't feel ready. Overwhelmed, she pressed her hands against the bathroom counter. Her pulse pounded against her temples and Tess took a deep breath and closed her eyes. *You can do this. It's going to be fine.*

She turned toward her purse lying atop the bed. She walked out of the bathroom and reached into the large bag, feeling the small pills that had spilled onto the bottom at yesterday's crime scene. She found the opened bottle and put all but one of the pills back inside before replacing the lid. She lifted the pill to her mouth but paused when her fingers reached her lips. She couldn't afford to be out of it tonight at the EverChange meeting.

But her heart continued to race, no matter how much she willed it to slow down. She could feel the beginnings of a migraine being brought on by her rising panic. She took the pill and swallowed. She couldn't afford to be anxious tonight either. Colton might sense it. She needed to be relaxed.

She heard the front door open.

"Hey babe," Blake called.

She looked at the bottle of anxiety medication in her hand. She opened the top drawer of the dresser next to the bed and tossed the pill bottle in with her underwear. Blake walked into their room as she closed the drawer.

"Hi," she said, forcing a smile. She hated keeping things from him, but she also didn't want to have to explain her anxiety attacks.

"Wow," he said. "You look amazing." His eyes moved to the deep v-neck of her dress. "Did I forget we were going somewhere tonight?" He set his work laptop on their bed.

"Um...no. I'm going out with Chloe. She's picking me up in ten minutes."

"Oh? Where to? And how was your first day of your new, top-secret job?"

"It was fine," she said. The throbbing in her head was growing worse by the minute. She hoped the pill she swallowed would kick in soon.

"I saw that your resigning from homicide made the news. Who leaked that? The article made it sound like you're quitting the police force entirely. Is that something to do with your new job?"

"Yes. It's for my new assignment."

"So, where are you and Chloe going?" he asked when she didn't elaborate.

Tess turned and started digging through her jewelry box atop the dresser. "She's taking me to an EverChange meeting."

"What?"

When she looked up, she saw his demeanor had changed. He looked angry.

"I thought I told you Chloe still went to their meetings."

"I don't want you to go."

"I have to."

"What do you mean, you *have* to?"

She wasn't sure what to say without telling him her assignment, which she'd been specifically warned not to do. She realized that had been a bad choice of words. But she didn't want to lie to him.

"I mean, I *want* to. Chloe says the meetings have been really good for her, and she thought maybe they could help me deal with Chris's death."

She could see in his eyes that he hadn't bought it. Not for a second. He knew she had no interest in joining an organization like EverChange. And he knew she was lying to his face.

CHAPTER TWELVE

"You're the one," he said, looking at her in disbelief.

"I'm the one *what?*"

Tess looked strikingly beautiful, and Stephenson recognized the resemblance she bore to both Colton Everett's late wife...and new girlfriend. But Tess was a terrible liar. *How could they send someone undercover into a high-stakes operation who is such a terrible liar?*

"The intelligence unit is sending you in to join EverChange. You're the one."

She stared at him but didn't respond.

"You don't know what you're getting into. Everett is a sex-trafficking murderer. You'll be in way over your head."

"Excuse me?"

"I mean, I don't want you going. I have evidence linking EverChange, and Colton Everett, to my new homicide case. It's not safe."

"Not safe?" she scoffed. "I'm a detective. Same as you."

"*I* wouldn't go in there like this. I don't think you realize what Colton Everett is capable of."

"Or is it that you don't think I'm capable?"

"It's not that. But you have no experience going

undercover. How can they send you into such a dangerous organization? I mean, besides the fact you look like his dead wife and new girlfriend."

Tess narrowed her eyes at him as a knock sounded at their front door.

"That's Chloe. I have to go." She grabbed her purse from the bed. "If things go to plan, I might not be home for a while."

He reached for her arm. "Please don't do this."

"I have to go," she said, pulling out of his reach. "Thanks for the vote of confidence."

"Tess, wait!" he called as she went to the door. But she didn't turn back.

He sank back onto the bed after hearing her leave. How long had she known about this and kept it from him? For the first time in their relationship, he wondered if he really knew her at all.

CHAPTER THIRTEEN

"Thanks for picking me up," Tess said after climbing into her sister-in-law's Land Rover. She put on a smile, forcing her fight with Blake to the back of her mind.

"No problem," Chloe said, smoothing the sleeve of her faux fur coat. She pulled out of Tess's driveway. "I'm just glad you finally wanted to come back to one of these."

Chloe kept her eyes on the road, but Tess watched her expression turn serious.

"I just saw the news about your resignation."

"Sorry you had to find out that way. I didn't realize it was going to make the news. The job just became too much of a reminder of Chris's death."

Chloe nodded and glanced in her direction. "I think coming to an EverChange event is the perfect place to start fresh. I'm sure you'll find a job that you love where you aren't surrounded by death...and murder."

"Thanks. I'm sure I will too." Tess let out a deep breath. Fortunately, her cover wasn't far from the truth. "So, what marina are we going to?"

"We're not. Everyone's meeting at the home of Rachelle Morales. You know who she is, right?"

"The founder of that software company?"

"Datix, yeah."

And, Tess thought, according to Forbes, one of the richest women in America.

"Anyway, Colton wanted to keep the event really exclusive, so he's bringing his yacht over to her private dock on Lake Washington. There's going to be a lot of very well-known and wealthy guests there tonight, so he thought it would be best for everyone to meet at her house, rather than a marina."

Tess stared out the window as Chloe drove across the floating bridge over Lake Washington. The calm waters were surrounded by waterfront mansions peeking through evergreen trees. Behind them, the sun was nearing the horizon, leaving only about an hour of daylight.

"So, what does Blake think about you coming to an EverChange meeting after you dated Colton?"

Tess turned to her sister-in-law. "I didn't date him. I went on *a* date with him." She felt annoyed that her relationship with Colton was being exaggerated for the second time that day.

"Okay. So, Blake doesn't mind?"

"Um...I've never mentioned it."

"You never told him you went on a date with Colton Everett?"

Shortly after they crossed the bridge, Chloe took the exit for Medina, one of the most expensive zip codes in the country. The area was home to a few of the richest people in the world.

"No. It was only one date. I've just never thought to bring it up."

They passed a jogger with a Labradoodle before Chloe

turned onto a narrow street lined with tall, neatly-trimmed hedges on either side. Chloe turned around a bend before coming to a gated drive. She braked behind a Bentley that was stopped at the gate.

A muscular man in a black suit opened the gate for the Bentley and motioned for Chloe to pull forward. She stopped beside him and lowered her window.

"Name, please?" he said.

"Chloe Richards."

He checked his phone. "Have a nice night," he said, giving her a quick nod before pressing the button to open the gate.

"Thank you." Chloe pulled forward inside the large circular drive and parked next to the Bentley.

The women stepped out onto the cobblestone drive and made their way to the mansion's front entrance. From the other cars parked in the drive, Tess realized the guest list was much wealthier than she had imagined. She and Chloe walked past a black Bugatti that Tess guessed was worth more than her home.

"I feel like I might've underdressed," Tess said, looking down at her long-sleeve fitted minidress.

"You look amazing," Chloe said as they climbed the concrete front steps.

The home's over-sized double doors were propped open and a beautiful woman held a tray of champagne flutes as they entered. They each took a glass before they were greeted by the home's owner.

"Welcome," she said warmly.

Tess recognized the short, dark-haired entrepreneur from her recent cover on *Forbes* magazine.

"I'm Rachelle. I don't think we've met before."

"I'm Chloe Richards, and this is my sister-in-law, Tess."

Chloe was only a couple inches taller than Rachelle, and Tess felt like a giant next to the women in her four-inch heels.

An attractive couple stood next to the software founder, and Tess recognized the man as a pitcher for the Seattle Mariners whom she'd seen in the photo with Colton earlier that day.

"Have you met Antonio and Ariana?" Rachelle asked.

"Yes, we've been at a couple of meetings together," Chloe said.

Tess shook hands with the pair as Chloe introduced them.

"Well, I think everyone else is already on the yacht if you all want to follow me."

The women's heels resounded against the marble floors as Rachelle led the way through her home. They stepped out onto an expansive concrete patio that opened to a manicured green lawn leading down to the lake. There was just enough daylight left for Tess to admire Mount Rainier in the distance. The women stepped carefully in their stilettos as they followed Rachelle down the uneven, stone walkway through the lawn to her large private dock.

Colton's yacht dwarfed the floating structure, sticking out well past the dock's bigger moorage space. Tess guessed the sleek white luxury vessel to be almost one hundred feet long and could only imagine what it cost.

Live music resounded from inside the boat as they climbed aboard. They moved inside the yacht's glamorous interior where most of the guests were gathered. Servers wearing all white carried trays of hors d'oeuvres through the well-dressed crowd.

Tess kept her eyes peeled for Colton as Chloe introduced her to a few of the guests. Tess made her best attempts at small talk, trying to seem as though she had something in common with the wealthy cult followers as the vessel pulled away from the dock. Indoor and outdoor lighting illuminated the waterfront estates as dusk settled across the sky.

There were fewer than fifty people on the boat, and she noticed the crowd was mostly women as they cruised along the shoreline in the direction of Mount Rainier. Tess recognized one of the male guests as a Seattle City Council member.

The sky had darkened when the yacht cruised underneath the Interstate-90 bridge that connected Mercer Island to downtown Seattle. Chloe and Tess's conversation with Adriana, the wife of the Seattle Mariners' pitcher, was interrupted by the sharp clinking of a glass. Their heads turned to the corner of the room, where Tess saw Colton for the first time since their date two years earlier.

He stood on a chair, holding a butter knife in hand and a champagne glass in the other. He smiled as everyone turned his way. He was one of the most attractive men Tess had ever seen. He wore a dark suit with no tie. The top few buttons of his dress shirt were left undone. His dark wavy hair was a strong contrast to his light blue eyes.

"I want to thank you all for coming tonight to celebrate the success of EverChange and the tremendous impact it's had on our lives." He scanned the faces in the room as he continued. "And our—"

Tess felt a tingle down her spine when his eyes rested on hers.

"Communities," Colton finished, keeping his eyes fixed

on Tess.

Tess recognized the face of Avery Hill, Colton's fiancé standing on the floor beside him. Avery's eyes followed Colton's stare. They narrowed when she saw he was focused on Tess, making Tess wonder if Avery knew that she and Colton had gone out once.

Colton held Tess's gaze for a moment longer as he went on to boast about all the great things EverChange was doing for individuals, corporations, and the environment. Tess felt herself blush when he broke eye contact and went back to scanning the room.

"Colton was totally staring at you!" Chloe whispered into her ear.

"He was probably just surprised to see me here."

Chloe pursed her lips and gave her a look that said, *yeah right*. "I don't think that's why he was staring."

As they went back to listening to Colton's speech, Tess caught Avery staring at her before she looked away.

"If there's anyone here tonight who isn't yet a member of EverChange, please come see me or Avery and we would love to answer any questions and help you become a member. *And,* if I could have your attention for another few minutes, I've asked my good friend, Antonio Ramirez, if he would say a few words about how EverChange has impacted him. Whether you're a baseball fan or not, you probably know him as the record-breaking pitcher for our Seattle Mariners. He's a great man who does a lot for his community, and I'm thrilled to have him as our newest board member for EverChange."

The room applauded as Antonio approached Colton. Colton stepped off the chair and joined in on the applause.

"Thank you," Antonio said as the clapping subsided.

"It's such an honor to be on the board of EverChange."

Tess took the opportunity to study the room while everyone's attention was diverted to Antonio. Every eye was fixated on the athlete as he told the story of how EverChange helped him to become the best version of himself.

Tess leaned toward her sister-in-law as Antonio's speech was winding down. "I want to join."

Chloe looked up at her. "Really?"

Antonio's voice filled the room. "So, cheers to Colton and to EverChange!"

Applause filled the room once again as Antonio raised his glass in the air before taking a drink.

"Yeah. I need a change. Maybe EverChange can help me find a new direction in life."

"Wow, I'm so glad," Chloe said. "I was afraid you wouldn't take this seriously." She grabbed Tess by the elbow. "Come on. I know someone who's going to be glad to see you."

Tess followed Chloe through the crowded space to the bar where Colton was standing. He looked to be having an intense conversation with an attractive brunette when they got close to him. He placed his hand on the young woman's shoulder after eyeing Tess.

"Excuse me," she heard him say before he stepped toward them.

"Glad you could make it tonight, Chloe," he said.

He was taller than Tess had remembered. Probably close to six-foot-five.

"Thank you," Chloe said.

He turned to Tess. "I see you've brought a friend."

"Yes. You remember my sister-in-law, Tess?"

He extended his hand. Tess pressed her palm against his and he held his gentle grip around her hand a moment longer than necessary.

"It's lovely to see you again." His eyes looked intensely into hers.

"She wants to join EverChange," Chloe said.

"I'm so glad. Why don't we get a drink and you can tell me what's brought you back while we sign the paperwork."

"Sure."

He stepped in between Tess and Chloe, placing his hand on the top of Tess's back.

"What would you like to drink?" He led Tess toward the bar, leaving Chloe standing by herself.

"I'll have a Pinot Gris."

"We'll have two glasses of Pinot Gris," he said to a young woman behind the bar.

He grabbed a folder from the end of the granite countertop and motioned to the barstool next to him. "Have a seat."

Tess slid onto the white leather barstool as he took a seat beside her. The pretty bartender set their wine glasses in front of them.

"It's been awhile since you've come to an EverChange event. What makes you want to join now?"

Tess took a sip from her drink. "Well, my brother died last summer—"

"I'm so sorry. I read about that in the news."

"Thank you. Ever since his death, I've been...struggling. And having a hard time at work. I just quit. Today, actually. I need a change." She paused, giving him the opportunity to speak. But he didn't. "Chloe's been saying really great things about EverChange, and I was hoping it could help me redirect my life."

"You were a cop, right?"

She nodded. "I've been working as a homicide detective for just over a year."

She was half expecting him to flinch, but he didn't show any reaction to her profession. "Well, EverChange will help you become the greatest version of yourself, which will empower you to make the right decisions moving forward."

Tess smiled, wondering how people could buy into this nonsense.

He set a stapled stack of papers in front of her. She smelled the subtle scent of his cologne as he leaned in closer. "This is a non-disclosure and confidentiality agreement as well as our membership agreement. We have all our members sign it. It means that anything you share within the group or at any meetings is entirely confidential." He handed her a pen.

Tess scanned the text on the pages as she flipped through them. *And that anything I see or hear at EverChange is also confidential.* She signed at the bottom of the last page and handed him back his pen. His fingers touched hers when he took it from her.

"When's the next meeting?" she asked.

His eyes moved to something or someone behind her before he met her gaze. "We don't plan them in advance, but we'll contact you a few days before the meeting. We try to meet a few times a month."

He glanced behind her again. This time, she turned and followed his gaze. Avery watched them with a dark expression from the other side of the room.

"Excuse me," he said, standing from his chair. He picked up the form she'd signed and slid it back into the folder before placing it behind the bar. "It was wonderful seeing you again, and I can assure you that EverChange is going to really positively impact your life." He held out his hand a second time, holding hers for a lingering moment, just like he'd done earlier.

She watched him walk toward Avery, who eyed Tess disapprovingly before turning away. Tess left her wine glass at the bar, knowing she wasn't supposed to mix alcohol with her anxiety medication. Tess made her way through the attractive crowd until she found Chloe laughing with Rachelle.

"Well, how'd it go?" Chloe asked. "Colton acted like I was invisible after I told him you wanted to join."

"It went well. I signed the paperwork to join."

"That's great!" Chloe said.

"Yes. I joined tonight too," Rachelle said. "I've just heard such great things coming out of EverChange."

"Me too," Tess lied.

They were almost back to Rachelle's dock when Tess spotted Avery climbing the stairs to the upper deck. For the last hour, she'd looked for another opportunity to speak to Colton, but he was nowhere to be found. She didn't want to wait until the next meeting to make a closer connection to him. She needed to get inside his Whidbey Island compound and find out what was going on. If Blake was right, at least one woman had been killed. That investigation couldn't afford to wait. If she couldn't connect with Colton, maybe she could connect with Avery.

Chloe was deep in conversation with a few of the other guests, but she didn't want her coming to look for her.

"I'll be right back," Tess told her as she moved past.

"No worries," Chloe said.

Tess felt a chill from the cool night breeze when she stepped out onto the open upper deck. She was happy to see Avery was alone. Tess had done her research in the short amount of time she'd had before the party and knew she and Avery had something in common. Other than their looks. Something they didn't share when Tess had met her the first time.

Avery leaned over the railing, staring at the shoreline. She turned in Tess's direction as she walked across the deck. Tess came to a stop next to Avery and pressed her lower back against the railing. For a moment, the two women stood in silence.

"I read an article about you tonight," Avery said. "About you quitting your job."

"Oh, yeah. I didn't realize it was going to make the news when I resigned." She let out a sigh. "There were reporters outside my home earlier today. I just want to be left alone."

"I'm sorry about your brother."

Tess nodded. "Thank you."

"I was surprised to see you here tonight. It's been a long time since you've come to an EverChange meeting. But I know losing someone you love can cause you to see life differently."

"You've lost someone?" Tess asked.

"Yes. My sister. She died in a car accident five years ago."

"I'm so sorry. I never knew that," she lied.

"Yeah. It was really tough at first. And it still is sometimes, but EverChange has helped me."

"I joined tonight. I hope it can help me too."

Tess could feel Avery's eyes on her as she stared at the floor of the boat. She brought tears to her eyes. "I just couldn't work in homicide anymore. I feel like a failure for quitting, but it was too much of a reminder of what happened to him. It's been almost a year since his death, but sometimes I feel like it was just yesterday." She wiped the tears that streamed down her face.

Avery's cold hand touched her arm. Tess brought her eyes up to meet hers. "I just feel so...lost."

Avery enfolded her in a hug.

It's working, Tess thought. The yacht pulled up to Rachelle's dock as Tess returned Avery's embrace.

"Avery, you coming?" Tess recognized Colton's voice from the top of the stairwell.

"In a minute," Avery said. "You can wait for me by the house if you want."

"All right."

Tess heard Colton retreat down the steps. It was easy to see who called the shots in their relationship. Tess was glad she'd sought Avery out.

"Chris's murder is being re-tried next week. I can't bear to go through it again. I'm already overwhelmed with anxiety about it."

Avery pulled back and put her hands on Tess's shoulders. "We're going to help you. EverChange will give you the strength you need to get through it."

"I need to get away from all of this." Tess looked down at a few laughing party guests sauntering off the yacht. "I can't even bear to go home."

The two women stood in silence for a moment before Avery spoke.

"Colton has a place, an estate, on Whidbey Island where we allow some of the EverChange members to live. It's mostly for members who want to completely immerse themselves into EverChange away from their previous lives.

It's a place where members can really get grounded and discover who they really are without the distractions of day-to-day life. We normally only invite people who have been heavily involved in EverChange for a while, but, if you're serious, I could talk to Colton. Maybe it's what you need to deal with the loss of your brother."

Tess looked into Avery's eyes. "Thank you. Yes, that sounds like exactly what I need right now."

"Just give me a few minutes to convince him." Avery led the way back downstairs. "We're heading there tonight. You can ride with us."

"There you are!" Chloe called from across the yacht when they reached the bottom of the steps. "I was starting to think you fell off the boat."

Chloe was one of only a few guests still on the yacht.

"We were just having a chat," Avery said.

"Well, let's go," Chloe said, looping her arm around Tess's. "They're continuing the party inside Rachelle's."

Avery walked ahead of them as they got off the boat.

Chloe leaned into Tess once Avery was out of earshot. "What were you talking to her about? I didn't picture you two liking each other."

"She's nice actually. Once you get to know her."

"Hmm." Chloe smiled. "Whatever you say."

They were almost back to the house when Tess spotted Avery and Colton at the edge of Rachelle's patio. They looked like they were having a heated argument. Tess slowed her pace to hear what they were saying.

"But she's a cop!" Tess heard Colton say.

Tess strained to hear what Avery said next over the breeze coming off the lake.

"We can keep an eye on her," she heard Avery say as

Chloe gave a slight tug on her arm.

"Aren't you coming inside?" Chloe asked.

Colton looked up at the sound of Chloe's voice. "Fine," he said to Avery before he strutted past her into the mansion.

Avery turned and gave Tess a nod of victory as Tess followed her sister-in-law back into the party.

CHAPTER FOURTEEN

Stephenson checked his phone for the umpteenth time as he lay in bed unable to sleep. It was almost one a.m. and Tess still hadn't come home. He sat up.

What had she meant by, *If things go to plan, I might not be home for a while?* Was she expecting to go to Colton's Whidbey Island compound *tonight?* That seemed unlikely.

He called her for the second time in the last hour. When he'd called her the last time, her phone rang before going to voicemail. This time it didn't ring at all. She must've turned it off. He ended the call without leaving a message. He tried Chloe, but she didn't answer. He decided to leave her a message.

"Chloe, it's Blake. I'm just trying to reach Tess. Her phone seems to be off, and she hasn't come home yet. Can you give me a call when you get this? Thanks."

He flung back his comforter and swung his legs over the side of the bed. He ran his hand up the back of his short blond hair and thought about calling Chloe's husband, Tess's older brother Nathan. But he was on his annual fishing trip in Canada with a few of the other Seahawks before they started their off-season training. He wouldn't know if Chloe had come home yet.

How could the Intelligence Unit send his wife undercover into EverChange with no experience? He knew they had picked her because of her looks and her connection to EverChange, not because of her skill running covert operations. It wasn't safe. Plus, he knew she'd been having a harder time with Chris's death and murder trial than what she'd been admitting. He wasn't sure she was in the right frame of mind to be doing this, even if she were properly trained.

He flicked on his bedside lamp and went to the closet to get dressed. He checked his phone screen another time after putting on jeans. He needed answers. If he couldn't get them from Tess, he'd get them from the person who put her in harm's way.

The lieutenant's motion-censored lights came on as Stephenson approached the front door of her two-story home. He rang the doorbell before banging his fist against the door three times. He noticed the lights come on inside a room over the garage before the curtains split open.

A moment later, he heard footsteps trod down the inside stairs. Wallace swung open the door after unlocking the deadbolt. Her dark, shoulder-length hair was splayed in a mess of different directions as she glared at him through her puffy eyes.

"What the hell?"

"That's what I want to know," Stephenson said. "Why would you send Tess undercover into EverChange without any experience? Just because Colton Everett likes tall blondes doesn't make her qualified. You could get her killed."

Heavy footsteps sounded on the stairs behind the lieutenant.

"Honey?"

Stephenson looked beyond Wallace to see a bald man wearing a t-shirt and boxer shorts come to a stop halfway down the staircase.

The lieutenant waved her hand without turning around. "It's fine. I'll handle this." She crossed her arms and narrowed her eyes at Stephenson. "You have no right to come to my *home* and question my decisions. And how do you know she's going undercover? She wasn't supposed to tell you."

"She's a terrible liar. And I'm her husband."

"I didn't know you were married."

"It's new. And she's been in a fragile state since her brother's murder. You know about that, right?"

"Yes."

"How could you send her to spy on Colton Everett without any training? Don't you have your own people who do that kind of thing? There's no way she could be prepared for this. She told me if things go to plan, she might not be home for a while. You're trying to get her inside his Whidbey Island compound aren't you? He's going to find out she's a detective. She's been in the news about Chris's murder."

"He already knows. Didn't she tell you they dated?"

"What?"

"Back when she was going to EverChange meetings. She didn't tell you?"

"She told me she went to a few meetings. Not that she dated him."

"Well, maybe she's a better actor than you know. She'll do just fine at EverChange."

Stephenson was at a loss for words. He couldn't imagine Tess not telling him this. Maybe the lieutenant was making it up.

"Look, I understand you're upset. For that reason, I'm going to do you a favor and let you leave without incident. But I don't appreciate you using the department's resources to find my unlisted address. Don't *ever* come here again. Understand?"

Stephenson fixed his jaw and let out a breath through his nose. "Yeah."

He heard her re-lock the deadbolt after she slammed the door shut.

CHAPTER FIFTEEN

Tess looked out the window from the backseat of Colton's helicopter as they neared his Whidbey Island estate. Colton and Avery sat in the front seats, with Colton effortlessly piloting the small chopper. After they crossed the bay, Tess could see the lights from the huge mansion as Colton smoothly maneuvered the helicopter onto the helipad adjacent to the large estate.

Tess knew her heart would've been racing if it weren't for the clonazepam she'd taken earlier. She hadn't really thought she'd be coming to the compound tonight. Once the blades had stopped, she climbed out after Avery and followed them up the paved walkway to the rear of the mansion.

She looked up at the tall stone structure. Its roofline and stone-walled exterior reminded her of an English castle. As they got closer, she noticed some of the windows were stained glass.

The home was dimly lit when they stepped inside. And quiet. Its interior seemed to match the mansion's Gothic Tudor exterior.

Tess was surprised there was no one in sight. She was

half expecting the home to be filled with young women wearing matching gowns, holding hands, and chanting their allegiance to Colton. But, standing in the living room of Colton's mansion, she realized that was ridiculous. EverChange drew people in by promising hope and appearing normal on the surface. She was going to have to get in deep to find out what was really going on inside the billionaire's cult.

Her eyes moved across the wood-paneled walls, crown molding, and the beautiful arched windows centered with ornately-stained glass.

"This place is amazing," Tess said. "How old is it?"

"Thank you," Colton said. "Let's have a seat before we go upstairs." He motioned toward two blue velvet couches that faced each other in front of a large stone fireplace.

Tess took a seat on the one Colton had pointed to, while he and Avery sat down across from her. Tess crossed her long legs after sitting, aware of her skirt hiking up to the top of her thighs when she sat down.

"The house was built in the early 1900s by a railroad developer who dismantled a sixteenth-century Welsh castle and had the structure shipped to Puget Sound to be reconstructed. So, much of the home is over five hundred years old."

"Wow." Tess looked around the room, pretending to be engrossed in the interior decor rather than the fact she was in the heart of Colton's cult.

Colton slipped his hand over Avery's leg while his eyes drifted to Tess's thighs. "We just need to establish some ground rules now that you're here."

"Okay." Tess pulled on the hem of her dress, trying unsuccessfully to cover more of her legs.

"This is a place for reconnection with your inner self," Colton said. "We don't allow our guests any outside influences, including cell phones or other possessions. We want you to be free to let go of all distractions that can keep you from reaching your full potential. Are you willing to do that?"

"Of course."

"Great. Then we'll need you turn over your purse before we go upstairs. And this doesn't mean that you'll be permanently cut off from the outside world. We have a landline you can use if you need to make any essential contact with someone outside. It's in a secure part of the house, and if you need it, you just need to ask.

"You'll have a roommate, but not tonight. The other girls have already gone to bed. So, we'll give you your own room for now. Some of our practices might seem strange at first, but trust us, they've proven effective in helping people reach their full empowerment."

Avery held out her hand for Tess's purse after they stood from their seats. "We're glad you're here," she said.

Tess forced a smile. "Me too."

Tess passed two medieval knight statues before she followed Colton and Avery up the wooden staircase. The house was eerily quiet as Tess followed them down a long hallway lined with Renaissance paintings and medieval weaponry. Tess slowed as she observed the antique daggers and swords that hung from the walls.

Colton turned and followed her gaze.

"These all came with the house," he said. "The original owner was a collector of medieval artifacts. Most of them were found in the Welsh castle before it was torn down and shipped here."

Tess's eyes drifted to an ornate double-headed axe.

Colton smiled and pointed at the crescent-shaped blades. "That's a battle axe. Cool, isn't it?"

"You could do some real damage with that," Tess replied.

They passed several doors on either side of the hall before Avery stopped at a doorway. It creaked as she swung it open. Avery flicked on the light and stepped inside.

Tess followed, taking in the large four-poster wooden bed and tall velvet curtains that lined a large window. The room was big, and there was plenty of room for the two overstuffed chairs that sat in front of the unlit fireplace.

Avery opened a drawer from the bedside table and pulled out a short silk nightgown. As she laid it atop the bed, Tess noticed the Valentino label on the inside of the gown. A shiver ran down her spine when she realized it looked exactly like what Andrea Morris had been wearing when her body was found.

"The clothes you're wearing are a part of your old life. We'll get you new things to wear while you're here." She held the nightgown out to Tess. "I'll take your clothes before I go."

Tess took the gown and started to walk toward the en suite bathroom.

"Sorry," Avery said. "But I'll have to watch you undress. I just need to make sure you don't keep anything."

Like a wire, Tess thought. She turned toward the opened doorway and saw that Colton was gone.

"It's just us," Avery said.

"Fine." Tess stepped out of her heels before pulling off her dress. She hadn't worn a bra. "Even my underwear?" she asked as she set her dress on the bed.

"Yes."

Tess tried not to roll her eyes. She pulled the nightgown over her head before she took off her underwear and laid them on top of her dress. Avery picked Tess's clothes off the bed and touched Tess's arm before leaving the room.

"This place and EverChange is going to be exactly what you need to deal with the loss of your brother and find a new way in life."

"I hope so."

"You'll be amazed at what you find within yourself while you're here." Avery paused when she reached the doorway. "I'll see you in the morning."

Tess stared at her bedroom door after Avery closed it behind her. *What am I doing here?* She and Blake had been married less than a week. *Maybe I should've resigned and gone to the retrial of Chris's murder rather than start an undercover assignment.*

But she had a job to do. Women's lives were at stake. She just hoped she could make Colton and Avery trust her enough to let her see what was really going on inside this secluded castle...before anyone else got hurt.

CHAPTER SIXTEEN

Tess felt as though she'd just fallen asleep when she was awakened by the strident creak of her bedroom door. She sat up in bed and watched a petite blonde girl bring a silver breakfast tray into her room.

"Morning," the girl said as she set the tray down on the coffee table in front of the fireplace.

"Morning." Her eyes followed the girl as she marched across Tess's room and briskly pushed the thick velvet curtains to either side of the tall arched window. Tess squinted from the early-morning sunlight that flooded the room.

"I'm Portia." She reached for the set of clothes that were folded under her arm and laid them on one of the overstuffed chairs, along with a small black shopping bag.

"Hi, I'm Tess."

"I know. I've been assigned to serve you today."

Serve her? "Do you work here?"

The girl wore sneakers with black leggings and an oversized pink sweater. She was thin, maybe a little too thin. Even from across the room, Tess could see that she was strikingly beautiful, and there was a vague familiarity about her.

She laughed at Tess's naivety. "No. I live here. Same as you now. Serving is part of the EverChange way."

"Oh. Right." Tess rolled back her comforter and swung her legs over the bed. "Well, thank you for breakfast. Have we met before? You look familiar." Tess wondered if she could have been on the yacht last night.

"I don't think so. You might know me from Instagram."

The famous fashion blogger registered in Tess's mind. She'd seen something recently about Portia hitting over 100 million Instagram followers.

"But it just got to be too much," Portia added. "So, I came here." Portia smiled. "Anyway, you'll find all the toiletries you need already in the bathroom. What size shoe do you wear?"

"Um...a nine."

"I'll put a pair of shoes for you by the front door. We're meeting downstairs in front of the house in a half hour. Don't be late."

She was out of the room before Tess could say anything else. She yawned and made her way over to the silver breakfast tray. She added some creamer to the mug of black coffee before eating the egg-white omelet and half a grapefruit that had been neatly arranged on a white plate. She held up the clothes, which looked to be her size. Leopard leggings and the same oversized sweater Portia had worn, only Tess's was black.

She recognized the Nordstrom label on the small shopping bag Portia had set next to the clothes. She looked inside and saw it was full of high-end makeup products, more than twice the price of what she normally wore. After pulling on the new clothes, which fit perfectly, she picked up the grapefruit spoon and sank into the fabric chair. *Here we go.*

Tess found a box of new Nike running shoes by the front door as Portia had said. She slipped them on before pushing open the solid, hand-carved oak door to the front porch. She recognized Avery standing in the large circular drive next to a sculpted fountain, along with Portia and about ten other pretty young women. They all wore the same leggings and oversized sweater as Tess, just in different colors.

"Good morning," Avery said as Tess approached the group.

"Good morning," Tess said.

"This is Tess," Avery said to the girls. "She joined us last night."

A chorus of *hellos* resounded from the girls. Tess scanned their faces and realized she was standing among a group of very famous women. She recognized almost all of them. The lieutenant had warned her that she might find some celebrities at the castle. But not to this extent. A reality TV star from southern California stood to Tess's left. Among the women across from them was a retired tennis pro, an ex-Olympic skier, and a celebrity chef. Tess's jaw dropped when she spotted Summer Channing, an Oscar-winning Hollywood actress.

Tess tried to brush off the wave of insecurity that rushed over her. "Um, hi. It's great to be here."

"You'll get to know everyone soon," Avery said. "This is only half of the residents. The other half are having a session with Colton this morning."

Tess wondered what the *session* was comprised of.

"Since this is your first day with us," Avery continued. "I thought we'd start with what we call a *trust walk*. We do these from time to time. And, as you probably weren't aware...today is Colton's birthday. We'll be kicking off the celebration this afternoon. Follow us."

Tess walked behind Avery and the other girls across the damp, freshly mowed grass. They moved around the side of the castle to the back of the house. The rear of the property was just as well-manicured as the front. They moved past a multi-colored rose garden as Tess followed the women along a stone pathway through the acres of manicured lawn. The estate was completely private, surrounded by tall, tightly-spaced fir trees on either side.

Tess brushed away a strand of hair that had blown across her face. No one spoke as they moved swiftly through the landscaped acreage toward the bluff at the edge of the property. Tess looked across at the mainland on the other side of the choppy bay. Avery stopped and turned to face the group when they neared the cliff. She nodded to Portia, who withdrew a few pieces of dark fabric from her pocket and began passing them out to some of the girls.

"Those of you who are familiar with this exercise know it's all about building trust. Since trust is one of the principles EverChange is founded upon, we want to nurture and grow our trust of our fellow members and leaders with the organization. Portia is handing out blindfolds to half of you. When you receive one, put it on.

"Then, you'll be paired with the person next to you. For this exercise they will be your master and you will do everything they say without question or hesitation. They will lead you in a number of different directions and you must follow exactly where they tell you to go. Understood?"

"Yes." A chill ran up the back of Tess's spine as the girls answered in unison.

Tess watched a few girls put on their blindfolds before Portia held one out toward her. Tess accepted the black piece of fabric and slowly covered her eyes before tying it behind her head.

"Everyone have on their blindfolds?" Avery asked.

"Yes," the other girls chanted.

"Okay. Your master is going to start leading you. You'll know they're your master because they will be the voice closest to you. It might seem confusing at first, since there will be four masters speaking, so you will have to focus on discerning the voice of your master from the others. Let's have everyone wearing a blindfold take a big step forward and then we'll start."

Tess fought the panic rising in her chest as she stepped forward, knowing they'd only been a few feet from the cliff edge to start with.

"All right go," she heard Avery say.

"Step to the right," a voice said in her ear.

"Take a step forward," another girl said, not quite as close as the girl in her ear.

Tess took a deep breath and stepped to the right as she willed her heart rate to slow.

"Step forward."

Tess took a small step, wary of the bluff edge right in front of them.

"Now step left," the same voice said.

Tess obeyed, but slowly and carefully now that she was probably only a foot from the edge. She hadn't looked over the edge before putting the blindfold on, but from the level of the water, she guessed the beach was more than a hundred feet below.

"Step back."

"Step right."

"Step forward."

There were so many voices speaking at once, Tess had trouble discerning which was closest to her.

"Step forward," a voice said again, this time closer to her ear.

Tess took a deep breath. Was this some sort of initiation into the cult? Or had they somehow learned of her role with the Intel Unit and planned to trick her into walking off the edge of the cliff?

"Step forward." The voice was louder and more authoritative than it had been before.

This is so stupid, Tess thought. *I'm not walking off the edge of a cliff out of some blind obedience.* But she had to make them believe she trusted them. And that she was there because she believed EverChange could help her.

Tess lifted her foot and carefully felt the ground in front of her. Slowly, she shifted her body weight forward and lifted her other foot and placed it next to the other. A strong breeze blew against her and she fought to maintain her balance with the blindfold. She leaned backward slightly, knowing she was possibly inches from the edge of the cliff.

"Okay, everyone." Tess recognized Avery's voice coming from behind. "Well done. You can take off your blindfolds."

Tess reached her arms behind her head and untied the knot she'd made in the silky fabric. Her eyes widened as the blindfold slipped down her face. She looked straight down at the rocky beach below. She jumped back. The toe of her shoes had been less than an inch from the edge. If she'd stepped any farther, she would've fallen to her death.

She felt her face flush with anger. She looked around. All the other girls were a few feet back. She shot a look at Avery, who watched her with a flat expression. Tess's breathing quickened.

She wrestled with the desire to march over to Avery and ask what kind of sick game she was playing. Was she playing chess with people's lives for enjoyment? To feel powerful? To keep the girls *obedient?*

She turned to the girl she'd been partnered with. The one who'd instructed her to nearly walk off the edge of the cliff. It was the reality star Tess had recognized earlier. Violet something. Her fiery red hair blew across her face from the wind. Violet's green eyes betrayed no emotion as she tucked her hair behind her ear.

Had she been ordered to make Tess walk off the edge? Or were they testing her? Trying to get inside her head?

"Now we'll switch roles. Hand your blindfolds to your master, and you will lead them."

Tess caught Portia staring at her as she handed the blindfold to the pretty redhead who'd almost killed her. Unlike the others, Portia's eyes displayed concern. When their eyes met, Portia was quick to look away. She accepted a blindfold from her master and put it on.

"Okay, masters," Avery said once the other half had their blindfolds in place, "you will now lead your servants just as they did to you. Starting now."

Tess leaned into the pretty redhead's ear. "Step back."

The girl obediently followed all of Tess's directions without hesitation over the next few minutes. Unlike her partner, Tess was mindful of giving her a wide berth from the deadly drop. Tess stopped in her tracks when she saw

Portia standing nearly as close to the edge as Tess had been. Portia's master leaned into Portia's ear and said something Tess couldn't quite hear. Tess recalled watching the tall brunette on TV, playing at last year's US Open.

She watched Portia raise her foot in the air and step toward the cliff edge. Tess ran from where she stood as Portia started to bring her weight forward on her foot that hung in the air.

"No!" Tess yelled.

Portia fell forward as her foot disappeared beyond the cliff, searching for the ground. The weight of her body pulled her other foot off the grass as she toppled forward, over the edge. Portia let out a scream.

Portia's master stood still, making no effort to pull her back. Still a few feet away, Tess threw herself forward, pushing her feet off the wet ground for momentum. She grasped Portia's ankle with both hands a second before she hit the ground. The air was forced from Tess's lungs as her chest slammed against the ground, causing her to nearly lose her grip around Portia's leg. Tess felt a sharp pain in her shoulder as Portia's body fell against the edge of the cliff and the weight of her body became fully suspended by Tess's hold.

Tess let out a groan as she struggled to pull Portia up from the cliff. Portia silently pressed her hands against the sandy cliff, trying to push herself back.

"Someone help us!" Tess cried.

Tess was unable to look around as she lay face down on the grass clutching Portia's ankle with all her might. Fortunately, Portia probably only weighed one hundred pounds, but it was still a struggle for Tess to hold on. Tess got to her knees and pulled herself back, bringing Portia's foot a few inches onto the grass.

Her hands started to slip and she struggled to pull Portia back to the top.

"Help me!" Tess screamed.

Portia's ankle inched closer to the edge in Tess's grip as she grappled to maintain her hold. After what felt like an eternity, Avery knelt beside Tess and reached for Portia's other leg. Together, they slowly pulled Portia back to the top of the grassy ledge.

Portia slipped off her blindfold as she rolled onto her back on the wet lawn. Tears streamed down her face. Tess was breathing hard as she got to her knees. She glared at Avery as Portia wept.

"Why didn't anyone help her? What the hell is this? How can you call this an *exercise*? She could've died!"

Avery brushed off her hands before she rose to her feet.

"No master would tell their servant to walk over the edge. She must've heard wrong or heard someone else's direction. It's about focus, as well as trust."

Tess looked at Portia, who didn't argue with Avery as she choked back her tears.

Tess shook her head. "No. I watched her *master* whisper in her ear right before she walked off the edge of the cliff. And she made no attempt to save her or pull her back. She was going to stand there and watch her die. Like the rest of you."

Tess stood and took a step toward Avery. The long blonde hair of both women whipped across their faces from the wind. They were almost exactly the same height. Tess narrowed her eyes, waiting for Avery's response.

Avery pursed her lips and rolled her eyes. "Don't get so excited, *Detective*."

"I'm not a detective anymore."

Avery's eyes seemed to search hers. "Right. But there's no need to overreact. Portia's master, Monica, was trying to reach for her when you leapt between them. And Portia's fine." Avery looked at Portia, who sat up and wiped her tears with the sleeve of her sweater.

Portia nodded.

Avery looked back at Tess. "See? You don't always have to be the hero, Tess." Avery's lips formed a smile as she clapped her hands together. "All right, girls. Well done. Let's head back to the house."

The girls immediately walked in the direction of the old mansion. Portia got to her feet, brushed herself off, and jogged to catch up with the others.

Avery and Tess were left standing alone on the edge of the bluff.

"I know some of our ways might seem different and you may not understand them at first, but if you're going to stay here, I need you to try. You're going to have to let go of your old ways of thinking so you can embrace the enlightenment of the EverChange teachings. And that means trusting that we are not out to harm you. Or anyone else."

Avery turned for the house before Tess could respond.

Tess looked back at the torn-up grass at the edge of the cliff where Portia had nearly lost her life before she turned and followed Avery and the others back to the house.

CHAPTER SEVENTEEN

"You can all head to the library. Colton will be leading us in an advance training session," Avery announced when all the girls had returned to the house.

Tess followed the group of the women into a large room near the front of the castle. Wooden bookcases covered the walls from floor to ceiling. Colton sat on a tall stool next to a podium on one side of the room.

Rows of antique wooden chairs had been set up to face him. They were already half-filled with young women, all intensely focused on Colton. Tess's eyes widened when she recognized one of them as a supermodel who'd recently starred in a movie. Tess noticed they were all wearing the same leggings and sweaters as the girls in Tess's group. Tess didn't recognize any of them as the governor's daughter, but she couldn't quite see all of their faces.

Colton looked incredibly attractive, as usual. His wavy hair was perfectly groomed and his navy turtleneck accentuated his blue eyes. The girls took their seats without a word, and Tess followed suit. She looked down their row at Portia, still blown away at the lack of emotion or response the other girls had to her near-death experience.

"Good morning, ladies."

Tess turned at the sound of Colton's voice. He flashed the group a charismatic smile.

"I want to speak to you this morning about our past lives. And how the discovery of who we used to be can help us attain a higher success in our present state."

It took Tess's total concentration not to roll her eyes. Or look around the room and see if anyone was buying this nonsense. But she knew, of course, they were. She forced herself to look neutral and pretended to listen to Colton speak about how he came to the revelation that he was a great conqueror in ancient times as her mind drifted to that morning's events.

"I've also been given a revelation about who some of you were in past lives."

Colton's words brought Tess's attention back to him. His eyes seemed to pierce hers.

"I'll be speaking with some of you later today to talk about your past life and how it could impact your future. But, for now, I want to talk to you about letting go of the past so you can embrace your potential." Colton's gaze drifted to the other women. "When I talk about letting go, I mean letting go of the things from your past that are holding you back. Fears. Resentment. Painful memories. Things you allow your mind to emphasize that actually cripple your present state."

His words brought her brother's murder to the front of her mind. She didn't need to see a psychiatrist to know that the trauma of his murder and her hatred for his killer, who'd yet to be sentenced, was the root of her current anxiety.

She could see how the women were drawn to him. And not just his looks. He had a way of making you feel like he was speaking directly to you in a room full of people.

"We have to take responsibility for who we are. Our actions. Our choices. Our state of mind. As long as you're blaming someone else for your current struggles, you'll never move past them. Chapter Six of your manual talks more about this, and I'd like you all to study that this weekend—if you're not too busy at my birthday party."

The room joined him in laughter. "That's all for now, other than I want to welcome our new house guest, Tess Richards. We're really glad you're here."

The room full of beautiful faces turned toward Tess as Colton stretched his open palm in her direction.

Tess nodded. "Thank you."

Colton broke eye contact with her and clapped his hands together. "All right, let's party!"

Cheers resounded throughout the room as the women stood from their seats and bounded through the library's double doors. Two men wearing suits had appeared on either side of the open doorway, each holding a tray of champagne glasses. The group members slowed to grab a glass as they exited the room. Tess followed suit, carefully lifting a near-full glass on her way out. She took a sip to keep it from spilling over as she walked.

"What did you think of the meeting?"

Tess turned to find Avery walking beside her as she followed the group upstairs.

"I thought it was really helpful." *If you believed it.*

Avery nodded in agreement. "Good."

Pop music resounded through the windows from the back patio as the two of them rounded the landing in the middle of the staircase.

Avery turned in the direction of the beat. "Sounds like

Georgina is ready to start the party. She's an amazing DJ."

"The supermodel?" Tess asked.

Avery nodded. "She's pretty well-known for it in L.A. She's done a ton of celebrity weddings."

Tess looked out the window before she followed Avery up the rest of the stairs. The pool cover was off and a large buffet had been set up on the patio. A group of men and women wearing black and white uniforms were setting up outdoor heaters, tables, and flower arrangements while Georgina bobbed her head to the beat behind a table next to the pool.

"It looks like they're setting up for a wedding," Tess said. Although she didn't have any of those things at hers a week ago.

Avery smiled. "We do this every year for Colton's birthday. The party lasts for the whole weekend. It's extravagant, but he's the whole reason why we're here. And we need to celebrate."

They reached the top of the stairs.

"I've moved your things to your new room. So, I'll show you where you're at and introduce you to your new roommate."

Avery stopped halfway down the hall. She was about to push open the solid oak door when two bikini-clad girls burst out of their room across the hall, laughing as they ran toward the stairs.

Tess felt almost jealous of their lightheartedness as their laughs echoed from the stairwell. Avery opened the door and Tess followed her inside her new room. Her roommate was faced away from them, tying her string bikini top as she admired herself in a full-length mirror. But Tess recognized her instantly from the carrot-red curls that cascaded down her back.

"Violet, this is your new roommate, Tess."

Violet's curls whipped through the air as she turned around. She looked as unhappy to see Tess as Tess was to learn she'd be bunking with the girl who'd told her to step onto the cliff edge. But Violet quickly attempted to mask her disappointment with a curt smile.

"Great." Violet slipped into her clear plastic heels and pulled on a long fur coat over her bikini. "See you at the pool." She strutted out of the room without another glance in Tess's direction.

"Don't mind her. She'll warm up." Avery motioned toward the king-size four-poster bed. "This is your side of the bed. I've laid out your party attire. Hope you like it. You can head to the pool after you get changed. And this is one of the few rooms that doesn't have a bathroom, but there's one right outside the room. First door on your left."

Tess glanced at the tiny bikini and mesh coverup lying atop the bed. "Um, thank you. But isn't it a little cold for a pool party?" Even June in the Seattle area could be a little cold for swimming. And it was barely April.

Avery let out a soft laugh. "Normally, yes. But not here. We heat the pool to a hot tub temperature for Colton's birthday weekend. And you won't be cold with all the outdoor heaters. It'll feel like a summer pool party."

Avery moved toward the door. "This is a weekend of celebration. The only thing I want you to do for the rest of the day is relax, have fun, and get to know some of the other castle residents. And that's an order."

Tess returned Avery's smile before she shut the oak door behind her. Tess picked up the small pieces of fabric that comprised her swimsuit.

She checked her reflection in the mirror after she pulled the mesh coverup over her white bikini. Not that it did much covering, since it was practically see-through. She was grateful for all the marathon training she'd been doing lately, which had added definition to her naturally athletic frame. She sighed, thinking how Blake would love to see her like this.

She looked like she could be on her honeymoon. She tried to push aside the guilt she felt for deserting her new husband less than a week after they were married. She grabbed her large black sunhat off the bed and headed for the door. She needed to stay focused on her assignment.

CHAPTER EIGHTEEN

Stephenson squinted through his sunglasses as he looked across the glass outdoor table at Parker's father, Curtis, on his second-story deck. Curtis was not quite sixty, but his deep frown lines and creases across his forehead and edges of his eyes made him look older. His neck and shoulders slumped forward as he sat. Curtis lived on the beach and, from where he sat, Stephenson had a direct view of the lighthouse on the end of the seven-mile Dungeness Spit that protruded from the mainland.

Stephenson normally enjoyed the two-hour drive northwest to Sequim, but not today. He was too worried about Tess. He'd been coming to the picturesque seaside town every summer for the last four years to run the North Olympic Discovery Half Marathon, which included a five-mile stretch along the shores of the Strait of Juan de Fuca, but this was his first time traveling to the town for work.

Stephenson looked out at the calm waters of the Strait of Juan de Fuca, which separated it from the Vancouver Island and the San Juan Islands.

Curtis followed Stephenson's gaze.

"On a clearer day, you can see Mount Baker beyond the

lighthouse," he said.

"It's a lot clearer than it was in Seattle this morning."

"Oh, yeah. We're in the rain shadow here, you know?"

Stephenson nodded politely. "Right."

"A lot of people don't realize this, but despite being close to some of the wettest rainforests in the country, Sequim gets almost the same amount of rainfall as L.A. Less than half of what Seattle gets."

"Huh. I didn't realize it was that much less."

"Don't tell anyone though. I like my peace and quiet out here." He cracked a smile for the first time during their visit, but it quickly faded. "So, you have some questions for me about my daughter's death?"

"Yes. Did you believe it was an accident at the time?"

"*Hmmph.* You're the first detective to ask me that. No, I never thought it was an accident. Still don't. But there weren't any witnesses. And they said all her injuries appeared to come from her fall." His lip quivered and he wiped away a tear that escaped under his sunglasses. "She fell over one hundred feet."

Stephenson gave him a moment to compose himself before he pressed further.

"Why didn't you believe it was an accident?"

"I never liked the guy. There was something about him I never trusted. But he always seemed good to her. Parker had been hiking since she was a little girl. She wasn't a novice. And I can't imagine she would've gotten so close to the edge of a cliff. Colton said he was taking her photo at the top of the peak and that she backed up too far and slipped over the edge." He shook his head and looked out at the ocean. "Not Parker. She knew better."

Curtis turned back to Stephenson. "And then, Colton

gets a new girlfriend that looks just like Parker only a month after she died. He knew her while he and Parker were married, but the police weren't able to prove there was anything between them." Curtis's mouth turned to a scowl. "He even offered me *money* as some sort of condolence after Parker died. Like money could ever bring back my little girl. That son of a bitch."

"When I went through your daughter's case file, it wasn't clear whether she and Colton had a prenup. Were you aware if they had one or not?"

He shook his head. "I know they didn't. Her mother and I both told her that if Colton had enough reservations about their marriage to ask for a prenup she shouldn't marry him. And that if he really loved her, really trusted her, he wouldn't ask her for one. A prenup, in my opinion, is like planning for divorce. And if you're planning for divorce, then you shouldn't get married. Marriage is about trust, you know?"

Stephenson nodded, reminded of Tess, and her never telling him that she dated Everett.

"Parker would never have signed one. I'm sure of it," Curtis added.

"Okay."

"Wait. Do you think he killed her because they didn't have a prenup? Are you re-opening her case?"

"I haven't re-opened it officially. And technically, her case is not my jurisdiction. However, Everett has come up in connection with a recent investigation, which led me to your daughter's case. I just want to make sure all possibilities were thoroughly explored."

"I can assure you they weren't. I asked them to re-open Parker's case after Colton was first seen out and about with his new girlfriend, but they wouldn't. They said all the evidence pointed to an accident." Curtis leaned back in his chair. "I almost hired a private detective, but my wife became ill and...I didn't want to put her through any more than we'd already been through. She died just over a year ago. Only three years after Parker."

"I'm very sorry."

Stephenson thanked Curtis for his time and followed him through the house to the front door. As they passed through the living room, Stephenson noticed more than one family photo where they all wore backpacks and hiking gear.

"You said Parker grew up hiking. But what about Colton? Was he a big hiker that you remember?"

Curtis turned around. "Colton?" He scoffed. "No. He grew up a pretty little rich kid. And mostly indoors from what I've heard. I was surprised when Parker told me he'd planned their hiking trip."

"Colton planned it?"

"Yeah. He knew how much she loved hiking. At the time, I thought it was nice gesture. Until we got the news that Parker fell. It was such a shock...I didn't really know what to think to be honest. Except that if one of them was going to fall, I would've expected it to be Colton. His story of how she fell made her seem so careless. And very unlike her."

They reached the front door, which Curtis opened for the detective.

"Thanks again for taking the time to speak with me," Stephenson said.

Curtis gripped Stephenson's shoulder before he could move through the walkway.

"You're the only hope I've had since those detectives closed Parker's case years ago. Promise me, please, that you won't stop looking until you find out what really happened to her?"

Stephenson nodded. "I promise," he said before stepping out into the afternoon sun.

CHAPTER NINETEEN

Tess took a sip from her second glass of champagne and sank lower into the heated pool, letting the warm water flow over her shoulders. The late afternoon sun was fading and being replaced by the castle's decorative outdoor lighting. She turned her head toward a loud splash in the middle of the pool, followed by laughter.

She watched Colton surface after being pulled off his floatie by Aspen, the Olympic skier famous for both her own world records and for having two retired Olympic skiers as parents. After pushing his hair from his eyes, he playfully pulled the Olympian against him and sank beneath the surface. When they came up for air a few seconds later, they both burst into laughter.

Colton climbed back onto his floating mat, and Tess couldn't help but smile as the other eight women in the pool flocked to his side. They were all holding onto a part of his king-size floating lounge chair as they pushed him around the pool, erupting with giggles every few minutes.

Could this be a sign of sex trafficking or just flirting? She wondered how Avery fit into all this. She didn't strike Tess as a woman who liked to share. From the looks she'd given

Tess the few times she'd caught Colton eyeing her, she'd appeared the opposite: possessive.

Tess scanned the patio until she found Avery lying on a lounge chair in her bikini under one of the large radiant heaters. Avery looked onto the scene in the pool with a smile as she drank her champagne. Apparently, she wasn't bothered by her fiancé's flamboyant display of affection for the other girls.

Tess spotted Portia reclining a few lounge chairs away from Avery. The look on her face was distant. Serious. She seemed to be the only one there not having a great time.

Next to the elaborate buffet of fresh seafood and tropical fruits, Georgina turned up the volume with the darkening sky and bobbed to the rhythm of her beat. A few girls jumped out of the pool to join the others who were dancing under the heaters. Tess noticed about a third of the girls had the same brand as Andrea on their lower back. The scar looked even more atrocious in person. It looked like an unhealed wound. Tess couldn't understand how any of them would choose to do that to themselves.

The water rippled in front of her and Tess was surprised to see Summer Channing lean against the edge of the pool next to her. It was hard not to be starstruck as Summer flashed her a warm smile of perfectly straight white teeth. She was even more beautiful in person than she was on the screen.

"They're really infatuated with him, huh?"

Tess followed her gaze to see one of the girls jump onto Colton's lounge chair with him as the others continued to move them around the pool.

So maybe he's not sleeping with *everyone*, Tess thought.

"I mean, don't get me wrong, this place and his teachings

have changed my life. And I think he's amazing." Summer finished her champagne and set her glass on the edge of the pool. "Just not enough to act like an idiot."

Tess laughed. "How long have you been here?"

The two women turned their heads away from the splash created by Violet's cannonball into the middle of the pool.

"I've been staying here the last four months, and it's been incredible. Given me a whole new perspective. Inner confidence and strength."

It was hard to imagine the Oscar-winning actress lacking confidence.

"But I've been following the teachings of EverChange for a lot longer than that. Colton and I met at a party a couple years back and he introduced me to the ways of EverChange. I attribute much of my recent success to his teachings."

Tess nodded, not sure how to respond. This place wasn't what she expected. Other than that morning's *exercise*, the estate felt more like a reflective, star-studded Playboy mansion than the cult castle she was anticipating. And, although she knew there was a chance she might run into someone famous at the party on the yacht, she presumed the women at the castle would be those that society wouldn't miss. Women who were seeking the kind of fame and success these women had already achieved. She'd expected these women to be vulnerable. Broken. Tess realized, as she stood next to one of the most famous actresses in the world, that she'd expected these women to be more like herself.

"I'll have to go back to L.A. soon. I start filming a new movie at the end of month, but I'm sad to leave.

"So, tell me about you. I heard Avery call you *detective*

earlier. Is that what you do?"

"Used to. Now I'm trying to figure out what to do with the rest of my life."

"Well, you're in the perfect place to figure that out."

"Hey, Summer," Violet called from across the pool where she clung to the side of Colton's floatie. "Who's the best male co-star you've ever had?"

Summer smiled. "On screen or off?"

Laughter and hollers resounded from Colton and the group of women who surrounded him. Even Tess couldn't suppress a giggle.

Summer enfolded her perfectly manicured hand around Tess's forearm and pulled her toward the stairs. "Come on. Let's dance."

CHAPTER TWENTY

Stephenson scrolled through Parker's case file on his laptop in search of Colton Everett's phone records that had been obtained during the brief investigation. When he returned from Sequim, he'd picked up a USB drive containing Taylor Neilson's case file from the King County Major Crimes office downtown. From the report, there was no evidence to suggest her death was anything other than an overdose, possibly accidental. Just like Amber had said in yesterday's early-morning meeting. But he did learn from her autopsy report that Taylor had the same brand as Andrea on her lower back.

His doorbell rang a minute after he found the phone records. He checked an app on his phone while he got up to answer it.

For a fleeting moment, he hoped it might be Tess. She'd escaped the compound after observing the depths of corruption within EverChange. But he knew as soon as he saw her sister-in-law on his phone's screen that it was ridiculous to think Tess would be back so soon. As he went to let her in, he realized she was his sister-in-law too.

Chloe smiled when he opened the door. Her arms were

bundled around the coat Tess had worn to the EverChange party. She stepped into the house before he had a chance to ask her in.

"Sorry I didn't answer when you called this afternoon. I was at the gym. After getting your voicemail, I thought I'd just stop by. Tess left her coat at the party last night. She's not here, is she?"

Chloe plopped onto the living room couch next to his laptop. He folded it closed before taking a seat next to her.

"No. Did you see I called you last night too? I was worried when she didn't come home."

"Yeah. Sorry. I thought she should be the one to tell you she was taking some time away. I don't even know how long she's planning on staying there. It seemed kinda spur of the moment. But she hasn't replied to my texts, and I'm wondering if she gave up her phone. Colton's place on Whidbey Island is for very intensive personal growth, which probably includes a detox from all things connected to her phone.

"I'm sure they'll give it back to her eventually," she added, seeing his frown.

"Did you know she dated Colton?"

Chloe scrunched her eyebrows together. "I wouldn't say they dated. They went on *one* date. Before she met you." Her hand swiped through the air like she was swatting a fly. "It was nothing."

She'd made him feel better and worse at the same time. At least Tess hadn't omitted that Colton was her ex-boyfriend. But why didn't she tell him they'd gone on a date when he mentioned EverChange's connection to his new homicide case?

"What's wrong?"

Stephenson leaned forward and rested his elbows on his knees. "I don't like her being there. I don't see how brainwashing is going to help her." He turned to his sister-in-law. "No offense."

She rolled her eyes. "None taken. People are always judgmental about things they don't understand."

Only he understood all too well the things going on within EverChange. Like murder.

Chloe put a hand on his shoulder before she stood from the couch. "Don't worry. Tess knows how to take care of herself. And she needs this right now."

Stephenson didn't respond, and Chloe turned to face him when she reached his front door.

"I know you think EverChange is fronting itself as a self-help group to scam money out of rich people. But it's not. They've helped a lot of people, and they do a lot of good. You'll see. Tess will be a changed woman when she gets back."

Stephenson sat back on the couch after Chloe closed the door behind her.

"I hope not," he said, opening his laptop and getting back to work.

CHAPTER TWENTY-ONE

Colton's birthday felt like a dream when Tess awoke the next morning. She sat up in the four-poster bed and looked around the room. It was definitely not a dream. She was alone in the room and could hear the faint sound of music coming from outside.

She smoothed her nightgown after getting out of bed. *Were they partying again already?* According to the downstairs grandfather clock, it had been nearly three a.m. when everyone returned to their rooms.

She looked around the room for a clock but didn't see one. She felt surprisingly rested after going to bed so late. She'd had trouble sleeping since her brother's murder. It usually took her awhile to fall asleep, only to wake up in the middle of the night, unable to get back to sleep before her alarm went off for work. But last night she'd slept like a rock.

There was a light knock on her door. She pulled it open to find Summer holding a silver breakfast tray with an omelet, mimosa, and coffee. A-list actress Summer Channing. Her new friend.

Summer flashed a warm smile. "I thought you might be

hungry. I brought this up from the poolside buffet."

"Wow. Thank you." Tess moved aside for her to come in.

Summer sauntered toward the fireplace, gracefully carrying the tray. She plopped down into one of the upholstered chairs after setting the tray on the coffee table.

Tess sat in the chair next to her. "I don't think I could've made it up the stairs without spilling that mimosa."

The movie star crossed her legs under her crocheted bikini coverup. "I did my fair share of waitressing before I made it big."

Tess smiled and reached for the coffee. Despite being a world-famous actress, Summer had a casual and unassuming air about her.

"Anyway, how'd you sleep?"

"Great. Better than I have in a long time, actually. Do you know what time it is?" From the way she felt, it was probably noon.

"It's almost nine. The party's just getting started down at the pool, which I should probably get back to. But I wanted to make sure you were settling in okay. Violet takes a little getting used to." Summer straightened her sun hat as she stood from her chair. "But don't worry, she'll come around. She was really close with her last roommate."

"Did she get moved to another room or something?" Tess tried to sound nonchalant as she took a bite of her omelet.

"She left. I guess she decided it was time to go back to her life outside of here. Violet hasn't spoken of it, but I could tell it bothered her."

"Does that happen very often? Someone leaving suddenly to return to their outside life? Everyone seems so happy here."

Summer paused when she reached the bedroom doorway. "There's been a couple leave in the time I've been here. But I've only been here four months. And I'll be leaving at the end of the week." She shrugged her shoulders. "I guess some of us have more outside obligations than others."

Tess emptied the small container of creamer into her coffee. She debated whether to probe further, wondering if Violet's old roommate was Andrea Morris.

"How long ago did she leave?"

But Summer had already stepped into the hall, closing the door behind her without an answer. Tess figured she probably hadn't heard her question.

Or she had, but Summer was hiding something.

Avery clinked a silver knife against her champagne glass as soon as Georgina stopped the music.

"Could I have everyone's attention please?"

Tess popped the last strawberry from her dinner plate into her mouth as the group turned silent at Avery's request.

"Colton, I love you." Avery extended her arm toward her fiancé.

Colton stood from his poolside lounge chair and accepted her outstretched hand.

Avery smiled up at him before she continued. "I was a mess before I met you. You saved me from myself. Showed me how great my life could be. I'm eternally grateful to you for showing me the way, and I have the utmost respect for all the good you do in this world."

Tess scanned the group as Avery spoke. It seemed that

all the castle residents were present, but none of them resembled Charity Green. And she wasn't sure how to ask about the governor's daughter without risking her cover.

"Thank you, my love." Colton leaned forward and kissed her softly.

Cheers resounded from the group of residents. Summer clapped in her seat next to Tess and Tess obliged. The cheering subsided as Colton pulled away from his fiancé.

Avery raised her glass in the air. "To Colton! Happy birthday to the greatest man I've ever known."

Tess clinked her glass with Summer's and took a drink.

"To Colton!" the women shouted in unison.

"And before I take Colton upstairs to give him what he really wants for his birthday...." Avery paused to allow for the laughter and hollers that erupted from the group. "In honor of the brilliant teachings of EverChange, we're going to go inside and break into small groups for a time of reflection and sharing. You'll be grouped according to your tiers. See you inside."

"What are tiers?" Tess asked Summer as they stood from their table.

Summer looked surprised by her question. "They're a part of our ranking system. You move up in tiers as you progress through EverChange."

"What tier are you?"

"I'm still a one, same as you." Summer's hand moved to her diamond earrings. "The tiers are awarded with jewelry to signify your advancement. Tier ones get diamond earrings, tier twos diamond bracelets, and tier threes diamond necklaces. Tier four is the highest, which is awarded with a diamond ring, but only Avery has that. I'm hoping to move up to a two before I leave for L.A."

"Tier ones are meeting in the library," Avery said when they reached the double doors off the back patio.

Summer looped her arm through Tess's as they weaved through the house. When they reached the library, they joined the three other women sitting cross-legged on the floor. One was Aspen, the ex-Olympian. Tess recognized the others' faces from the pool party but had yet to be formally introduced.

A log crackled in the fireplace that burned between the built-in bookshelves on the far side of the room. The group turned their heads to the sound of the library doors closing to see Avery moving confidently toward them.

Avery wrapped her black kimono across the front of her Louis Vuitton monogrammed bikini as she knelt to the ground in front of them. She leaned forward to hand Tess a paperback book.

"This is your manual. We study it daily. It's what will deepen your enlightenment in the ways of EverChange."

Tess turned the book over in her hand, noting the photo of Colton beaming broadly on the cover under the title, *The EverChange Way* by Colton Everett.

Avery clasped her hands together. "All right, let's get started." Her voice was softer than usual. "Since Tess has just joined us and the rest of you are still beginning your journey within EverChange, I wanted to share with you how EverChange radically changed me once I started putting Colton's teachings into practice. And how studying the manual can help you do the same."

Tess glanced at the closed double doors. She wondered what tier level Violet was.

"And if any of you would also like to share how you came to find your home within these walls, I'm sure Tess would love to hear your stories."

Tess forced a smile as she nodded, as if to say *Of course I would*.

"I was in a bad place when I met Colton." Avery's voice took on a serious tone.

As Tess's gaze shifted to the other women, listening intently to Avery's every word, it dawned on her that she hadn't seen Portia since the night before. But before she had time to dwell on it, Avery's words tugged at Tess's attention.

"My sister's death had been eating away at me for years. She'd been only seventeen when she was in a fatal car accident. I was battling severe anxiety and depression. And nothing I'd tried helped, not really. Therapy. Pills. It was like putting a Band-Aid over a bullet wound. I managed to function at work and keep it secret that I was dying inside. In fact, I still wonder if I hadn't met Colton when I did, if I would even be alive today."

Tess swallowed, not liking how much she related to what Avery was saying.

"Colton was in the beginning stages of starting EverChange, based on his years of studying the power of the human mind through a unique combination of eastern and western teachings. He taught me how to control my thoughts, rather than fall victim to them. And it saved my life."

Tess could see a change wash over the women at her mention of Colton. Not quite a smile, but a glassy-eyed expression. As if hearing his name cast some sort of spell over them.

Although, Tess couldn't quite blame them. She could see how they could be spellbound by him. She might even be too, if it weren't for Blake. It almost made her smile thinking of her new husband, and how he would never go for any of this *power of the mind* teaching. He'd always been mentally strong. It seemed like things didn't get to him like they did her. And it made her feel weak in comparison.

"I've been off all medication and free from anxiety and depression for over three years now. And it's all thanks to him."

Tess joined in with the others' applause of Avery's story, even though she felt silly clapping in such a small group. The others went around the circle and shared similar accounts and how EverChange had saved them. But none of their stories resonated with her quite like Avery's and the loss of her sister.

As the others spoke, Tess pondered Avery's words. She longed to be free from the guilt and anxiety that overwhelmed her mind and body. To be well. If only what EverChange offered was real.

"I never knew that about Avery's sister," Summer said as they walked back to their rooms after the meeting. She shook her head. "That's so sad."

Tess wondered whether to tell her new friend about Chris. She was grateful Avery hadn't mentioned it, and Tess decided not to tell her tonight. She didn't have the emotional energy. And she was afraid talking about his murder before bed might keep her up all night. Although she knew she probably wouldn't sleep anyway. It had been a fluke she'd slept so well last night. Sleeping two nights in a row was surely not bound to happen.

"Yeah, that is sad." Tess suppressed a shudder as they passed the medieval knight statues before climbing the oak staircase. Something about them gave her the creeps.

Summer turned her head before following Aspen into

their room. "I want to hear your story before I leave. How you ended up here."

"Okay."

"Good night."

"Good night," Tess said before pushing open the door across the hall.

Violet was already in bed. She lay atop the white duvet, reading her manual in an emerald green silk nightgown. A soft pink gown was draped across the bed on Tess's side. Her eyes didn't move from her book as Tess crossed the room.

Tess set her own manual on the nightstand before reaching for her nightgown.

"Hey," she said as she climbed into bed.

"I'm trying to study." Violet refused to look up from her manual.

Tess crossed her outstretched legs and opened the manual Avery had given her, pretending to read the first chapter. With Summer leaving at the end of the week, her secluded evenings with Violet would be her best chance of learning all that was going on inside these walls. Somehow, she needed to earn the girl's trust.

Tess was deep in thought as she stared blankly at her open book, flipping the pages every few minutes for appearances. After a few minutes, her thoughts drifted to Blake. She wondered how he was coping with knowing she was at Colton's castle. He'd seemed so livid when he figured it out. By now, someone within the department must have informed him they'd be sending someone under cover within EverChange in connection with his recent homicide case.

Without a word, Violet flicked off her lamp and rolled

onto her side, her back toward Tess.

"Did you see Portia today?" Tess asked after another minute of staring at her manual. "I didn't see her all day."

No response. Tess turned back to her book. A few minutes later Violet's breathing changed to rhythmic snoring.

Tess's thoughts moved to her brother, and she prayed his murder retrial would end in a conviction this time. She felt a familiar anxiety build in her chest the more she fixated on it. She turned to the chapter in the manual Avery had mentioned earlier to distract herself from Chris's trial. It was titled "The Power of Mindfulness".

Mindfulness is the practice of observing and controlling your thoughts rather than falling victim to them. You, and only you, have the power to control your mind. You are your thoughts. And you have the ability to change your thought patterns. When a negative and self-destructive thought enters your mind, you make a choice to either accept or reject it. The problem with most people today is that they don't realize they have a choice.

Close your eyes and envision your thoughts floating through the sky like a cloud. If the thought is positive, productive, and uplifting, capture that thought and dwell on that positivity. If the thought is negative and self-limiting, allow that thought to drift away. Give it no further attention. The way to eliminate negative self-talk is to fill your mind with positive thinking.

Tess kept reading. The chapter went on to list examples of positive and negative self-talk, including empowering and reassuring one-liners to focus on while one practiced ridding the mind of all negativity. By the end of the chapter, Tess found herself yawning. She set the book on her nightstand and turned out the light.

Since her brother's murder, she'd gotten used to lying awake in bed sometimes until the early hours of the morning. She closed her eyes and was immediately filled with a sense of doom about Chris's retrial. *If a jury let his killer off once, why wouldn't they again? She felt an equal amount of guilt for not being there.*

She opened her eyes and stared at the silhouette of Colton's manual on her bedside table. It was a bunch of crap. But, she figured, what was the harm in giving it a try?

"I refuse to accept these thoughts of anxiety," she muttered under her breath before repeating some of Colton's stupid feel-good phrases. "Everything is going to be okay. This situation will have a good outcome. My fears are irrational." She paused to let out another yawn. "My anxious thoughts are not grounded in reality. Chris's retrial will likely result in a conviction."

Her eyelids closed as she tried to recall more positive affirmations from Colton's manual. But before she could remember any more, she fell into a deep sleep.

CHAPTER TWENTY-TWO

Stephenson snapped forward in his desk chair on Tuesday when he saw Avery's phone records had finally come through in his email. He'd been waiting for them all morning. After Chloe's visit on Saturday, he'd spent the rest of the weekend poring over Parker's case file, particularly Colton's cell phone records that had been obtained during the brief investigation.

He'd found a few exchanges of text messages between Colton and Avery's cell numbers about six months prior to Parker's death. And there was one phone call between them that lasted over a half hour. Then, the texts and calls stopped until nearly a month after Parker died. Parker and Avery had also exchanged a few text messages in the months prior to Parker's death.

Avery had apparently run in the same social circles as Colton and Parker. Through a quick Internet search, Stephenson had found a photo of the three of them smiling at a charity event a few months before Parker's deadly fall.

It had taken some convincing the previous day to get a judge to approve the warrant for Avery's phone records. But, in the end, Stephenson had been able to persuade the judge that not obtaining these records during the initial investigation had been an oversight. And, that with Everett's recent connection to the murder of Andrea Morris, due diligence was required to ensure he wasn't a killer on the loose.

Avery had exchanged daily text messages and almost daily calls with an unregistered, prepaid phone number starting six months before Parker died. Stephenson went back to Colton's records and saw the exchanges began just days after his initial texts to Avery had stopped. He returned to Avery's records and scrolled through until he found when the texts and calls to the prepaid phone stopped. A month after Parker died. The last call between Avery and the prepaid phone was the day before she started receiving texts and calls from Colton again. Right around the time they were seen out in public together holding hands.

Although it confirmed his suspicions, it wasn't enough without being able to prove the prepaid phone belonged to Colton. And, even if he could prove it was Colton's, it didn't prove he killed Parker. But it was a start.

Stephenson checked his phone, hoping for some communication from Tess even though he knew without looking there would be nothing. He'd stopped trying to contact Tess after that, not wanting to risk her safety. But he needed to know that she was okay.

He clicked on Tess's contact photo and started to type a message before deleting it. He turned off his phone screen and set it back on his desk.

How long did they expect her to be there? And how was she going to get out once she learned what was going on?

He thought about going to see the lieutenant again, but he doubted that she would offer up any more information than what she'd told him Friday night. But the unknown possibilities were driving him crazy. His cell buzzed atop his desk.

It was Adams.

"What's up?" Stephenson turned around and looked at his partner's empty desk chair. He'd been the lead investigator of Chris's murder and was therefore required to attend his complete re-trial, which left Stephenson alone to investigate Andrea Morris's death.

"We have a short recess so I thought I'd check in to see how our new case is going."

Stephenson filled him in on what he'd learned from Avery's phone records.

"Sounds like you're on the right track. I haven't seen Tess since the trial started yesterday. I figured since she resigned, she would be here. Is she okay?"

Stephenson didn't see any point in lying to his partner. "She actually took a new job at the Intelligence Unit."

"Oh." Adams sounded surprised. "She's not the one they're sending undercover into the EverChange mansion, is she?"

Stephenson heard Adams let out a soft chuckle. He wasn't sure how to respond.

"You still there?"

"I'm here," Stephenson said.

"I meant that as a joke. I mean, she just started there. Right?"

Stephenson breathed into the phone.

"Oh man. It's her?"

"Yes."

"Wow. That happened fast."

You're telling me, Stephenson thought.

"Hey, I gotta get back to the trial. You doing okay with that? With her being there?"

"Yeah. Fine."

"Right. Okay. Well, she's saved my ass a few times. She knows how to take care of herself. I'll talk to you later."

Stephenson stared at his computer screen after hanging up. She *did* know how to take care of herself. That wasn't what bothered him. Just thinking about her staying undercover at that cult leader's mansion made his skin crawl.

Stephenson glanced at his watch before getting up from his seat. With his hands tied in investigating Colton Everett, there wasn't anything else he could do at the moment. Chris's trial would probably still be going for another hour or two that afternoon. He pulled on his suit jacket as he walked out of the Homicide Unit.

CHAPTER TWENTY-THREE

"I won't be coming back to the room for a while after dinner."

Violet looked at Tess through the full-length mirror in their room while she secured her diamond bracelet. She looked striking in her burgundy minidress and over-the-knee boots.

Tess met her gaze. She'd just returned from another tier-one group meeting where she'd surprised herself by opening up about her struggles dealing with her younger brother's death. Violet had hardly spoken to Tess in the three days they'd roomed together. Tess had tried to talk with her the night before, but Violet had rolled over and gone to sleep without a word.

Violet spun around. "I've been trying to achieve the next tier for a while, and tonight I'll have the opportunity to prove that I'm ready."

Tess recalled what Summer had told her about the tiers, which were basically a set of ranks within the cult. Members would attain the next level by proving they had developed a higher state of mind. This seemed to be proven in a variety of different ways, most of which were still unclear to Tess.

"What do you have to do?"

"One of the newer girls is going to get her EverChange enlightenment brand tonight. Colton asked if I wanted to do the brand as my final act of commitment to move up to the next tier."

"Can I come? Watch, I mean. I could even help you if you need."

Other than Portia getting told to walk off the cliff, Tess had yet to witness any torture or sex crimes against the girls. She assumed they were being cautious about what they allowed her to see since she was new, especially since she was an ex-cop. But if she was going to testify as an eyewitness against Colton and EverChange after this was over, she needed to see a lot more than what they were showing her.

"No, sorry. It's not something we really do for show. It's more an intimate moment of commitment. Avery will be there, plus the girl's roommate to help hold down her legs. And Avery needs to see that I can handle it on my own."

Tess wondered if the girls even knew the brand was the overlapping letters of Colton's organization, as well as his initials. "What does the brand look like?"

"It's a couple of Greek symbols. In English, it means *ultimate trust*."

Tess wondered how the girls could be so blind not to see the so-called Greek symbols were really the letters *EC*. A knock sounded on their door, signaling it was time for dinner.

"Okay. Let me know if you change your mind."

"Don't worry," Violet said. "You'll be getting your brand soon."

Tess had no intention of getting a brand. She prayed that

wouldn't be necessary to maintain her cover. "How long has she been here?"

"Who?" Violet asked as she opened their door.

"The girl who's getting branded."

"About four months or so, I think. But some girls do it sooner."

Violet nodded toward the garment bag and shoe box laying on their bed. "You better get changed for dinner. It won't look good to be late."

Tess moved toward the four-poster bed after Violet stepped into the hall. Inside the garment bag she found a Gucci one-shoulder minidress in her size. There was a note from Colton next to the Christian Louboutin shoebox asking her to wear them to dinner. She lifted the lid to find suede over-the-knee boots similar to the ones Violet was wearing.

Tess stepped into the short dress, guessing her outfit cost close to her monthly salary as a detective. The dress was tight and she managed to only pull the zipper halfway up her back. She exhaled, trying to shrink her ribcage as she tugged at the zipper again. But the angle was awkward. The fastener didn't budge. She let out a sigh of frustration and moved across the suite to the floor-length mirror.

"The clothes fit okay?"

She jumped at the sound of Colton's voice. Tess spun around. Colton was impeccably dressed in a fitted black suit. He closed her door and took a few steps toward her.

"I didn't hear you knock," Tess said.

"I didn't. Sorry if I startled you." He held out a small jewelry box as he moved toward her. "I wanted to give you these. They're your tier-one earrings. I thought you might want to wear them to dinner."

Her fingers brushed his as she accepted the box. She cleared her throat. "Thank you."

His eyes moved to her reflection in the mirror. "You need some help with that?"

"With what?"

He flashed her a knowing grin. "Your zipper."

"Oh." She didn't want to say yes and be his damsel in distress. But it didn't seem she had a choice. Unless she wanted to go down to dinner with a half-zipped dress. Reluctantly, she turned her back toward him. "Thanks."

He stepped closer and gently moved her long hair to the side. She felt his breath on her neck as he pulled her zipper to the top of her dress with one smooth motion. His hands came to rest on her shoulders as he locked his eyes with hers in the mirror. She resisted the urge to move away from his touch.

"I don't know about you, but I regret we only went on one date. And I know I'm with Avery now, but I feel like we never gave ourselves a chance."

Tess ran her fingers atop the felt jewelry box as he held her gaze.

"Anyway," he continued. "I'm really glad you're here." His palms fell away from her shoulders and he turned for the door.

"Me too," she said, realizing there was more truth to her words than she cared to admit.

He turned back after he opened her door. "See you downstairs."

A few minutes later, Tess stepped into the hall and followed a couple of girls moving toward the stairs. They both wore long sleeve minidresses, similar in style to the one Tess wore, except different colors.

This is so weird, she thought.

Tess trailed behind the girls all the way to the large formal dining room downstairs. The table was set with fine china and crystal glassware, fully adorned with candles and flowers from one end to the other. Each place setting had two wine glasses, already filled with a white and a red.

Place cards had been set on each plate. Most of the girls had already taken their seats as Tess moved along the table to find her name. She walked all the way down the long table before finding her seat. It was next to the empty chair on the end, which she saw was for Colton. She guessed the empty chair across from her was meant for Avery.

There was only quiet murmuring as Tess looked around at the other women. There were about twenty of them.

"Who prepares this?" Tess asked the girl next to her.

"We do. We all take turns serving in different ways around the house."

She didn't look older than twenty. Tess's heart went out to her. There was something in her eyes that reminded her of Portia. She glanced around the table but didn't see her.

She hadn't seen her since Saturday and was starting to get concerned. Before their small-group meeting, she'd asked Summer about it, but Summer assured her Portia was resting and would be feeling better in another day or two.

Colton and Avery entered the room, arm in arm, and all the girls stood to their feet for the king and queen of their castle. Tess mimicked their respect, pushing her chair back a moment later than everyone else.

"You may be seated," Colton said when they got to their chairs.

How do they think this is normal? Tess thought.

Throughout the dinner, Tess noticed that none of the

girls spoke unless spoken to by either Avery or Colton. Colton and Avery made small talk throughout the dinner, asking Tess how she was settling in and telling everyone about their afternoon flight.

Tess caught Colton staring at her more than once during the meal. His eyes drifted up and down her body until she caught his stare and he would revert his gaze to his plate. Whenever Tess looked across at Avery, she quickly averted her eyes, as if she hadn't noticed her fiancé's wandering eyes. Even though she had.

Tess admired Avery's diamond necklace and noticed about half the other girls wore something similar. The large diamond on Avery's left hand is what distinguished her. It glimmered in the candlelight as she stabbed at her salad.

She looked for Portia throughout the dinner but couldn't quite see every girl on her side of the table. At the end of the dinner, Colton excused everyone from the table. A few of the girls stayed behind to clean up, while everyone else left the dining room. As Tess followed the girls out of the room, she was sure she didn't see Portia.

She turned to Avery. "Where's Portia?"

"Oh. She wasn't feeling well tonight. I'm sure she'll be back to normal in another day or two."

Seeing the concern on Tess's face, Avery placed a hand on her arm. "Really, it's nothing to worry about."

Tess nodded. "Okay."

Tess watched Violet disappear through the doors of the library as she followed the other girls in the direction of the stairs. She went to her room and waited a few minutes before stepping back out into the hall. She tiptoed quietly down the stairs in her bare feet. When she reached the library, the double doors were closed. She pressed her ear against the hand-carved oak and recognized Avery's voice on the other side.

Tess took a deep breath and twisted the handle of the solid wood door. Violet, Avery, and Aspen's heads jerked in her direction when the door creaked as it swung open.

The overhead lights were off, but the room was lit by a few lamps and two large candelabras set up on either side of what looked like a massage table. Tess's heart sank when she recognized the blonde woman atop the table. She was blindfolded and her dress was pulled up to her armpits. Violet stood to her side holding a cauterizing pen, while Avery stood over Summer's head. Summer's roommate, Aspen, was holding down her legs.

Tess needed to earn Violet's trust. But she didn't want any part in helping Summer get branded.

"You're not supposed to be in here," Violet said.

"I just wanted to help."

"It's fine if she wants to stay," Avery said.

"Thank you." Tess closed the door behind her, thinking she should've known it was going to be Summer. She was one of the few who didn't have a brand, and her time at the castle was coming to an end.

"Just don't get in the way," Violet said.

"I won't." Tess moved closer, coming to a stop next to Aspen.

"Ready?" Avery asked.

Summer nodded, but her chest moved as though she were hyperventilating.

"Okay, turn onto your stomach. Remember...." Avery dipped her head toward her. "This is your chance to show how strong EverChange has made you. To prove to yourself you can withstand the pain. If you can get through this, you can handle anything."

"Okay. Hold still." Violet pressed the cauterizing pen against the back of her hip, causing Summer's body to jerk.

"I said, *hold still!*"

Summer let out a cry of pain through clenched teeth as Violet pressed the cauterizer against her for the second time. Tess felt nauseated from the smell of burnt flesh. Violet bent over Summer, struggling to keep her hand steady as Summer inched her body toward the other side of the table.

Violet swore as the cauterizer slipped up Summer's back from her movement.

"Hold her down!" Violet yelled at Aspen.

"I'm trying!"

But Summer kicked through her roommate's hold.

"Stop! Please stop!" Summer cried.

"I'm not done yet. This will go quicker if you hold still."

Avery nodded at Violet to continue.

Summer writhed under the women's hold as Violet struggled for the next several minutes to burn the lettering into Summer's skin. It took all of Tess's willpower not to intervene and make them stop torturing her friend. Despite the room's cool temperature, Summer's back beaded with sweat. She groaned in agony as Violet once again pressed the cauterizing pen against her lower back.

Tess saw the color had drained from the Olympian's face, who was working to hold down Summer's legs. She looked like she was going to be sick. Aspen gagged before bringing her hand to her mouth. She turned just in time for her vomit to land on the floor and not Summer. Summer threw her legs off the side of the table.

"I'm almost done, Summer," Violet said. "I just need you to hold still for a few more minutes."

But Summer refused to bring her legs back onto the table.

"Here, I'll do it." Irritation filled Avery's tone as she held out her hand for the cauterizing pen. "You weren't ready for this."

"But I—" Violet looked at Avery with pleading eyes.

Aspen heaved again before she ran out of the room.

"I'll help you," Tess said.

She wrapped her arms around her friend's legs and swung them on top of the table. Tess fought against her every instinct as she pressed her body weight against Summer.

"Fine." Avery returned her hand to Summer's shoulder. "But this is your last chance, Violet. If you can't get the brand done in the next few minutes, I'm taking over."

Tess leaned forward. "Do it," she told Violet.

Violet pressed the cauterizing pen into Summer's back. Tess swallowed the vomit that rose to her own throat from the stench of burning flesh and Aspen's stomach contents that had spilled onto the floor.

Summer squirmed beneath Tess's hold as a fresh waft of burning skin filled the air. It was all Tess could do to hold on and not throw up.

"I'm done," Violet finally said.

The minutes had felt like an hour. Tess let go and stepped back. She could hardly look at the movie star, who cried through her blindfold, hating what she'd just helped do.

Summer reached her hand toward her freshly-seared flesh, but Violet swatted it away. Even in the dim lighting, Tess could see her skin was inflamed around the raised area of the brand.

"Don't touch it. We don't want it to get infected. Let me put a bandage on it."

Tess stared at the horrific wound on Summer's lower back. A hideous scar she would have for the rest of her life. It was barbaric.

"You did it!"

Avery's congratulatory tone made Tess's stomach roll.

Violet locked eyes with Tess. "Thank you."

"You're welcome," Tess managed to say while backing away and shoving the library door open. She shut it behind her before she ran down the nearest hall, hoping she could make it to a bathroom before her dinner came back up.

"You look pale. Are you all right?"

Tess looked up at Summer from her spot on the powder room floor. She hadn't heard her open the door. The actress had changed into her nightgown and looked like she'd recovered from her painful ordeal.

"I'm so sorry for helping them do that to you."

Summer smiled and sank to the floor next to Tess. "Don't be sorry! I should thank you. You helped me go through with getting my brand. I've been wanting to do that for a long time. Now, I'll move up to a tier two before I leave."

"You didn't seem like you wanted to. It looked really painful. And you'll have that scar forever."

Summer put a hand on Tess's knee. "It was painful. But now it's over, and I'm so proud I went through with it. My scar will be a constant reminder of my inner growth and strength. And, now I know I can withstand anything."

Tess looked into Summer's blue eyes and knew that she

meant every word.

"No one likes going through the pain of changing," Summer continued, "but once you've evolved into a better person, you wouldn't go back for the world." She offered Tess her hand after standing up. "Come on, it's late."

Tess took Summer's hand, wondering how this place could feel so wrong and so right at the same time.

CHAPTER TWENTY-FOUR

Stephenson folded the last of the laundry and began to put it away before heading to work. He'd gotten home early from his morning run and decided to pick up a little before he left. Without Tess to push him farther, he ran a couple miles less than he usually did. He was also exhausted from worrying about her and the unknown of what was happening to her inside Everett's compound.

His investigation into Andrea's death frustratingly stalled without being able to search the EverChange estate or process Everett's car. He'd looked into Colton's fiancé's past, which hadn't turned up anything significant. Avery had no criminal history and nothing to note other than a younger sister who'd been killed in a car accident when she was hit by a drunk driver five years earlier.

His thoughts drifted back to Tess as he opened her underwear drawer. He smiled at the unorganized mess as he placed a few pairs of neatly folded underwear inside the drawer.

Something rattled inside the drawer when he started to close it. He pulled it open again and saw the bottom of an orange prescription bottle sticking out from under her underwear. He lifted the bottle and saw it had been prescribed to her about four months earlier. He didn't recognize the name of the drug so he read the printed instructions on the side of the bottle. *Take one tablet every twelve hours as needed for anxiety.*

Anxiety? Since when was she having anxiety? He looked again at the date. Why hadn't she told him? He read the colored warning labels stuck to the side of the bottle. *Do not mix alcohol with this medication. Marked drowsiness may occur. Do not operate heavy machinery while taking this medication.*

She'd never said anything to him about having anxiety, especially not severe enough that she needed medication. Except she *had* brought up her brother nearly every day since his killer's mistrial. Stephenson remembered her saying last week that she'd been having a hard time with Chris's death. Maybe she'd been trying to tell him. And he hadn't been hearing her.

He stared at the pill bottle. *How often had she been taking these? And, how could she allow herself to go undercover if she was struggling with this? Did she need them?*

He pulled on his suit jacket and slipped the bottle into the inside pocket. He didn't care if he was risking his job, he was going to see Lieutenant Wallace, find out if she knew about this, and get an update on his wife.

He backed out of the drive in the early morning light, wondering how he could be married to someone who kept so many secrets from him. His anger grew toward the lieutenant as he sat in the early morning traffic. Although, she might've been right about one thing, which both reassured him and pissed him off. Tess was most definitely a better liar than he thought.

CHAPTER TWENTY-FIVE

"You're looking lovely today."

Tess turned at the sound of Colton's voice as she came out of the library from her early-morning group meeting. He beamed at her from the front door, wearing a fitted polo shirt and shorts.

"Thank you."

He motioned over his shoulder. "A few of the girls and I are going golfing. We have a nine-hole course on the property."

Tess spotted a golf cart parked beyond the front porch steps. Two women were already seated on the back of the cart. Giddy laughter broke out between them.

"You want to join us?"

"Actually, Tess and I were going to take a morning drive," Avery said.

Tess hadn't heard Avery come up behind her. Avery hadn't said anything to her about going for a drive. Tess shot her a questioning look, but Avery's eyes seemed to say *just go with this*.

"Do you mind if we take the Ferrari?" Avery flashed her fiancé a coy smile. "I promise I won't scratch it."

"All right. As long as you're careful." Colton's eyes remained on Tess. "And if you promise to give me a rain check on the golf."

Tess nodded. "Sure."

Avery grinned and grabbed Tess by the arm. "Great! Let's go."

Avery sped out of the compound after the guard opened the gate. Tess gripped the Ferrari's door handle as Avery shifted gears on the windy tree-lined road. When Tess had seen the Ferrari in the garage, she was surprised it wasn't a new model, but a classic. In mint condition.

"What year is this car?" Tess asked. She leaned into Avery from the speed of the turn.

"1962. Fortunately, it's had a few modern upgrades." Avery maneuvered the silver gearshift with ease as she pulled onto the island's two-lane highway. "It's a pretty rare model. There were only about thirty of them made and even fewer are still around today."

"No wonder Colton warned you to be careful with it."

"Yes." Avery smiled and shifted. "This gearshift pattern takes some getting used to. You'd think first gear would be on the top left, but it's not. It's reverse!"

"Well, you don't seem to be having any trouble."

"I've had some practice. Speaking of Colton, I know you two went on a date a couple years ago."

"Oh. It was nothing. It—"

"I know. And he's only interested in you *now* because he wasn't able to have you. Even if it was by his own choice. It's a total ego thing. Men always want what they can't have. So, don't get too caught up in his charm. He can be very persuasive when he wants to be. Although, I probably don't need to be telling you this. Chloe told Colton at the yacht party that you're dating a homicide detective."

They passed a parking lot on their left as Avery sped toward the Deception Pass Bridge. Tess gripped her door handle tighter as Avery drove onto the narrow structure that towered a couple hundred feet above the Sound.

"Anyway," Avery went on before Tess could respond. "I wanted to talk to you about something that really helped me deal with my sister's death. I'm not sure if I mentioned it before, but she was killed by a drunk driver."

"I'm sorry."

"Thanks. One of the EverChange teachings that helped me heal was choosing to forgive that driver. Who killed her. I hated him for so long, and it was eating me up inside. He died in the crash too, but I was angry he got the easy way out. He never had to sit in a courtroom and face up to killing my sister. You might say that he got what he deserved, but I was pissed he could never be brought to justice."

Tess thought of Chris's killer. If his killer wasn't convicted, Tess wasn't sure she could handle it. They reached the small island that separated the two spans of the tall bridge, and Tess was glad to feel the car slow. Avery abruptly pulled into a small parking area. Tess's head shot forward as Avery slammed on the brakes.

"Until EverChange taught me the importance of forgiveness," Avery continued. "Once I forgave him, all those negative feelings started to fall away. And although I will never stop missing my sister, I know now that I can choose the thoughts I allow into my head. And I don't have to live filled with bitterness and resentment. I can choose to be empowered and in control of the way I live my life." A cool breeze filled the car when Avery opened her door. "Let's go take in the view. The last time I was here I saw a couple harbor seals."

Tess followed her out of the car. She knew she'd built up an enormous amount of hatred for her brother's murderer. As they walked down the path toward the viewing area, Tess watched the turquoise water rip through the narrow strait under the bridge.

She thought about all Avery had said. It made sense. Except for giving EverChange credit for the act of forgiveness. Wasn't that from the Bible?

CHAPTER TWENTY-SIX

Tess examined the back of the castle's exterior as she followed the straight line of girls in a jog around the property. She and Avery hadn't stayed long at Deception Pass. When they had returned to the castle, Tess was surprised to learn her mid-morning exercise was literally...exercise. Avery led the group at the front, and Tess took up the very back of the group. She was grateful for her recent marathon training. She guessed they'd jogged a few miles so far on the private grounds, and she'd barely broken a sweat. She did most of her runs with Blake, and she missed having him by her side.

Her stomach growled as they crossed the back patio, reminding her that half a grapefruit and the egg white omelet she'd had for breakfast hours earlier had long left her system. She'd hardly had any carbs since she'd been at the castle. She'd promised herself that as soon as this job was over, she was getting a cheeseburger and fries.

Thanks to her recent marathon training, she'd been able to focus her energy on surveying the security around the property. She'd seen three cameras on the front of the castle, one over the front door and one on each far corner. She looked along the rear of the castle but could only find one camera, over the double doors that opened to the patio from the main living room. There was another single door, which she guessed opened to the kitchen, but no camera.

Tess increased her pace to keep up with the group as they ran past the helicopter pad toward the trees that bordered the edge of the property. A light mist started to fall as they ran along the tree line toward the bluffs. Tess strained to look through the thick fir trees as she bobbed up and down, mindful of maintaining the same pace as the girl in front of her.

The front of the group had followed Avery to the left when they got close to the bluffs. Tess was glad to see they had a few feet between them and the edge and this wasn't another "trust" exercise. Before she turned, Tess found enough space between some branches to see a tall chain-link fence beyond the trees. According to the Intel Unit, the property was fenced on all sides other than the bluff.

Tess felt the first burn in her lungs over the next couple miles as they circled around the front of the castle before coming back to the bluffs. This time, she noted there were no security cameras on the sides of the castle.

As she jogged across the circular drive, Tess assessed the two-story lookout near the front gate where one of the girls seemed to be stationed at all times. She surveyed the brunette who leaned over the lookout railing. Tess's eyes were drawn to the rifle slung over her shoulder as she watched the girl peer through binoculars past the front gate in front of the castle.

In her time at the castle, Tess hadn't seen a single car drive past on the quiet road beyond the front gate. What made them think they needed an armed guard at the front gate?

She was out of breath when they rounded the castle for the third time, and she was glad when the group slowed to a walk. Colton waited beside the front door when Tess filed in behind the rest of the girls. Tess couldn't help but notice he looked his usual impeccable self in jeans and a fitted black shirt. She got a whiff of his cologne as she moved past him.

"Tess."

She turned.

"Avery's going to take me for a flight in the new Cessna I got her for getting her pilot's license. We have a small airstrip on the edge of the property. You're welcome to join us if you like."

"Oh, I didn't realize Avery was a pilot, too." But she couldn't go. The undercover detective would be arriving with the landscape team in less than an hour, waiting for her signal to stay or leave. "Thanks for the offer. But I think I'm going to study the assignment you gave me."

"Okay." He shot her a flirtatious smile. "I didn't take you as the studying type. See you when we get back."

Tess returned his smile before she turned for her room.

"And Tess?"

"Yeah?"

"If you have any questions about the manual or want to talk about anything, I'm here." He placed his hand over his chest. "Those earrings look great on you by the way."

She nodded. "Thank you."

She could feel his eyes on her as she walked away. She smiled to herself, thinking how much Blake would dislike him. And not just because Colton had been flirting with his wife. Blake would see through his charisma as a need for all the women's attention. He would recognize Colton's self-confidence as arrogance. And, Blake would probably be right. She was glad that the only woman her husband sought attention from was her.

The doors to the library were open, where some of the girls had gathered to do yoga after their run. Tess was glad to see Violet was among them. She didn't want to explain where she was going to her roommate.

Tess had been back to her room for less than a half hour when she heard Avery's plane take off. She moved to the room's large window and pushed the velvet curtain aside as she tilted her head upward. The noise from the plane's engine had traveled over the castle by the time she reached the window and all she could see was patches of gray clouds in the blue afternoon sky.

Her eyes moved to the landscape truck that was parking next to the large sculpted fountain in the center of the cobblestone circular drive. She checked her watch. They were right on time.

She watched a man step out of the passenger side and don a scarlet red 49ers hat. He was her contact. Tess moved away from the window and headed downstairs.

The rumble from a riding lawn mower filled the air when Tess stepped outside. She turned toward the noise. The man riding the mower along the side of the driveway wasn't wearing a baseball hat. Tess scanned the expansive front yard, aware of the girl staring at her from the lookout tower. She spotted the detective wearing the red cap trimming the hedges on the far side of the house.

Tess pretended to admire the grounds as she moved

slowly in his direction. The detective looked up when she got within earshot.

"Hey!"

Tess turned to see Summer coming down the front porch steps. The actress held her rolled-up yoga mat under her arm.

"Having a good day, ma'am?" the detective asked.

Tess bit her lip. If she said no, she could leave. Return home to her husband. But her job wasn't done. On the surface, it didn't seem there was anything criminal going on. She still hadn't seen the governor's daughter. It appeared the Intel Unit was wrong about Charity Green staying at the castle, which made Tess wonder if there were more things they'd gotten wrong about EverChange. But she needed more time to be sure.

The detective's eyes met hers.

"Yes," Tess said as Summer came to a stop beside her.

"That's great." He searched her eyes for a moment before returning the hedges.

"What are you up to?" Summer asked, ignoring the landscaper.

"I was just going to get some fresh air. Reflect on some things I read in the manual."

"I have to start packing. I can't believe I'm leaving tomorrow. I wish I could stay longer. I want you to come see me before I come back."

"In L.A.?"

"Yes! I can show you around the movie we're shooting. Even if you're not done with your time here, I'm sure Colton and Avery wouldn't mind you coming down for a short visit."

"Wow. Sure, yes, I'd like that."

Tess glanced at the undercover detective as Summer strolled back into the house. He'd be back in another week. Maybe by then she'd have enough information.

Tess kept walking in the direction of where she'd heard Avery's plane take off. She needed to be familiar with the entire property.

She moved across the lawn toward a thick row of fir trees that lined the side of the castle, assuring herself that her reason for staying was the investigation and not her newfound way of dealing with anxiety. Part of her wondered if Colton somehow knew her true reason for being at the castle.

She felt the temperature drop as she moved through the forested area, thick with evergreens that shaded the midday sun. A few minutes later, she reached a clearing.

It was about the length of two football fields, with a single paved airstrip in the center. An orange and white windsock fluttered at a forty-five-degree angle to the side of the runway. A white airplane hangar stood in the opposite corner of the clearing.

Through the tall trees that lined the property on the other side of the airfield, she could make out what looked like a chain-link fence. The height of it reminded her of a prison fence, although it was lacking the roll of barbed wire at the top.

The Intelligence Unit thought the fences and security were intended to keep the girls inside from escaping. But, given the celebrity status of some of the residents, it seemed possible Colton was simply providing them extra privacy.

Tess used her hand to shade her eyes from the sun as she looked to the sky, but Avery's plane was nowhere in sight.

"Can I help you, Tess?"

Tess jumped at the soft voice coming from directly behind her. She whipped around. The short brunette from the lookout tower stood less than a foot away. Up close, Tess recognized her as Camilla Ronaldo, a world-famous celebrity chef. Her rifle was still slung over her shoulder.

"No. Thanks, though. I'm fine," Tess said, taking a step back.

"Sorry, but you don't have permission to be out here."

Permission? "Oh. I didn't know I needed any. I was just going for a walk."

The chef took a step forward. "Colton would like everyone to stay at the house until he and Avery return. I'll walk you back."

She stretched out her arm as Tess stepped out of her reach.

"Tess, I need you come with me." There was an authority to her voice for the first time.

"Okay, I'm coming." Tess took swift strides back toward the house while maintaining a comfortable distance from the chef-turned-security guard. "So, I'm not allowed to go for a walk on the property?" she asked when they were halfway through the wooded area.

"Not unless you're with Colton or Avery. Or they've given their direct permission."

A small branch crunched under her foot. "Huh."

"It's only for your safety."

"Right."

They walked the next few minutes in silence.

"How many of you are there on the property?" Tess asked when the castle was in view.

"Guards?"

"Yeah."

"Only one at a time. We take shifts. But it's only when you're a tier three or above."

Maybe the Intel Unit had it right after all, and it was more about keeping the girls in rather than keeping people out.

Camilla stopped when they reached the circular drive. She stood next to the fountain and waited for Tess to go inside. The landscape truck was still there, but the men must have moved to the rear of the property. Camilla was still watching when Tess glanced back before closing the solid oak front door behind her.

Summer was filling two large suitcases with designer clothing when Tess came into her room. Aspen was reading the manual in an overstuffed chair next to the burning fireplace.

"How was your fresh air?"

Summer placed a perfectly folded blouse on top of her overflowing bag as Tess perched on the edge of her bed.

"It was fine. Until Camilla came and brought me back to the house."

"Oh, yes. They don't like us wandering too far off on our own. Sorry, I thought you knew. It's just for our safety."

Tess smiled. "Yeah, that's what she said, too."

Summer plopped onto the bed next to her. "I wish I didn't have to leave. I really love it here."

"Will you come back?" Tess asked.

Summer nodded. "But not until after we finish shooting the film. I hope I can stay grounded in EverChange's philosophies in the six months I'm away."

"I'm sure you will."

Summer wiped a tear from her eye and stood from the bed. "Well, I better finish packing before I change my mind."

"I'll leave you to it," Tess said. She turned when she reached their bedroom door. "Do you know what room is Portia's? I want to check on her."

Tess thought it was strange she hadn't seen her since Saturday. Even if she was sick.

Summer let out a loud sigh. "Portia's fine. Dramatic and dragging out her illness to avoid any sort of responsibility, but she's fine."

"I'll show you." Aspen tossed her manual onto the chair next to her and led Tess into the hall. She pointed to a closed door two doors down from Tess's room. "That one."

"Thanks."

Tess crossed the hall and knocked. After no answer, she tried the handle. The door opened freely with a soft creak. The four-poster bed was made and empty. Portia's roommate, Monica, was wrapped in a bath towel and blow-drying her hair next to the full-length mirror.

Tess caught the retired tennis player's eyes in her reflection. Monica turned off her blow-dryer and turned around.

"Did you need something?"

"I was looking for Portia."

The girl looked Tess up and down. "She's in the bathroom. Did you want me to tell her something for you?"

Tess scanned the room. It was just like the room she shared with Violet, and there was no en suite bathroom.

"No, that's okay. Thanks."

Tess heard Monica's blow-dryer come back on as she

shut the door. She moved down the identical oak doors that lined the hallway and pushed open the two she knew to be bathrooms. Both empty.

A sinking feeling filled her stomach as she walked back to her room. *Why were they lying about Portia?*

CHAPTER TWENTY-SEVEN

Stephenson's leg shook with anticipation as he waited for the lieutenant outside her office. He'd gone to see her that morning, but learned she was out of the office until this afternoon. He checked the time on his watch. *3:05.*

The lieutenant frowned when she appeared in the hallway. Her jacket was slung over her arm and she held a large Starbucks in her hand.

"What now, Detective? I thought you said everything you needed when you came to my house in the middle of the night." She marched past him toward her office door.

She left the door open, and he followed after her.

"Did you know Tess was on medication for anxiety?" He pulled the pill bottle out of his pocket and placed it with emphasis onto the lieutenant's desk.

She took a seat and looked up at him with contempt, refusing to lower her gaze to the prescription bottle. Stephenson knew he was crossing a line. But he was showing a lot of restraint by not telling her what he really wanted to say.

She folded her hands on her desk. "No, I did not. Because she never disclosed that to us. She willingly took this assignment. If she withheld something from us that ends up affecting the investigation into EverChange then she will be the one held accountable for that." She wrapped her fingers around the orange bottle and rolled it back toward Stephenson. "Not me."

"It seems to me that you threw her into a dangerous undercover operation without doing your due diligence. There was no time to prepare her for what you sent her to do. You didn't have the slightest idea of her state of mind. Do you have a plan for getting her out of there? And when?"

The lieutenant stood from her chair. "You're so out of line here that I should just tell you to leave. Your accusations don't deserve my explanation. But I understand your concern for your wife. Shut the door."

Stephenson remained standing after he pushed the door closed behind him.

"Detective Richards was given the opportunity to come home today. But she declined. It was completely her choice. We have an undercover detective liaising with her every week on the property, and she gives him a signal whether she stays another week or gets out. If she gathers enough intel, we plan to raid the property in less than three weeks."

She adjusted her blazer before she sat down and turned on her computer. "So, Detective, we're not as reckless as you may have thought."

Stephenson didn't know what to say. They gave Tess the opportunity to get out. But she chose to stay another week at Everett's mansion.

The lieutenant slipped on a pair of reading glasses. "Close the door behind you, Detective."

Stephenson picked up the pill bottle and slipped it back

into his jacket pocket before leaving her office.

CHAPTER TWENTY-EIGHT

Tess pulled at the hem of her Gucci minidress as she stood for Colton and Avery entering the dining room. She'd been one of the last to arrive at the enormous table, and she'd examined every face that was already seated on her way to her place. No Portia. She was sure.

"You may be seated," Colton said after he and Avery arrived at the head of the table.

They made small talk with Tess throughout the main course, and Tess refrained from asking about Portia. But something else also bothered her. When Colton's eyes met hers toward the end of the dinner, she took it as an opportunity.

"Why do you feel the need to have an armed guard by the front gate? I mean, the property already seems very private and secure."

Silence fell over those seated around them, including Avery, who stared at her with wide eyes from across the candlelit table. Tess remembered reading in the manual that EverChange followers were not to question its ways, because acceptance was the only way to true enlightenment. They were obviously not used to being questioned about anything they did.

Avery used her cloth napkin to dab her lips. "I don't think it's your place to question our security measures."

Colton held up his hand. "Avery, please. It's fine."

Avery watched him with a look of disdain as he took a drink from his wine. Her eyes followed the hand he placed on Tess's forearm. Tess made a conscious effort not to pull away.

"I can see how having an armed guard at the gate might seem extreme. We are a peaceful group, abiding within the laws on a very private piece of property. However, the world has never accepted what they've perceived as *radical thinkers*. And what they don't understand, they distrust. It might seem hard to believe when we're an organization centered around helping people, but there are a lot of people who would like to take us down.

"Look at Martin Luther King, Jr., Gandhi, JFK, Julius Caesar. What the world doesn't understand, they fear. And what they fear, they try to eliminate. So, I feel that it is my duty, as your leader, to keep you safe."

Avery's eyes were still fixed on Colton's hand as he patted her arm and stood from his chair.

"If I could have everyone's attention."

The entire table went silent as every head turned in his direction. Tess watched him pull three Harry Winston jewelry boxes from his suit pocket.

"We have three women tonight who've shown they are ready to progress to the next tier. I have the honor of awarding you with the jewelry to serve as a reminder of your level of achievement. Violet, you are now a tier three, congratulations."

Tess joined in with the applause from around the table.

"Summer, you are now a tier two. We are going to miss you greatly when you leave us tomorrow."

"Thank you," Summer mouthed from her seat next to Avery.

"And Tess, you are also now a tier two."

Avery's fork slipped from her hand and clanged against her plate. Colton grabbed Tess's hand and lifted it from the table.

"You showed outstanding loyalty and commitment by assisting Violet with Summer's branding and, thus, helping Summer find her inner strength."

He let go of Tess's hand and placed a jewelry box in front of her before moving around the table to hand a similar box to Summer and Violet.

Tess opened her box to reveal an elegant white gold diamond bracelet. She'd never worn anything like it in her life.

"Here, let me help you."

Tess turned toward the athlete sitting next to her. She extended her arm for Monica to fasten the bracelet onto her left wrist.

"Thanks." Tess noted the tennis pro wore an identical bracelet to hers.

Tess admired her bracelet after Monica secured the clasp. She watched Avery force a smile when Colton returned to his seat. For the rest of the dinner, Avery nonchalantly rearranged the food on her plate, throwing in a laugh for good measure every once in a while when something funny was said. But there was no mistaking what Tess had seen in her eyes when Colton gave Tess the bracelet: hatred.

Tess paused at the door to her bedroom and watched Colton lead Monica toward his room at the end of the hall. Avery held their bedroom door open and closed it behind the three of them.

Tess followed Violet into their room, who didn't say a word to her until after they turned out their lights. "Thanks for helping me last night."

Tess had almost been asleep. She opened her eyes and saw Violet's silhouette lying on her back, staring up at the ceiling.

"You're welcome."

Violet rolled onto her side and propped herself up with her elbow. "No one has ever become a tier two without getting branded."

Maybe that's why Avery looked so shocked when Colton gave me the bracelet.

"What did you give for collateral?"

"What do you mean?"

"Before you progress to a tier two, you're asked to put forth collateral to prove your loyalty and devotion to EverChange. You didn't have to do that?"

Tess wasn't sure what to say. She wondered why Colton was giving her this special treatment. Was he messing with her? Did he know her real reason for being at the castle?

"I'm not sure. What sort of collateral?"

"You'd be sure if you did. It would be something like nude photos, the deed to your home, or joint access to your bank accounts. Mine was a video of me saying horrific stuff about the other cast members of my show and the producers. They're never going to show it, but it would ruin my career if they did. It's just to prove your commitment to

EverChange."

"Are you…serious?" She couldn't imagine how these smart, successful women would agree to that.

"Yeah. They didn't ask you for anything like that?"

"No."

"Huh." Violet rolled onto her back. "No wonder Avery looked so pissed when Colton gave you the bracelet."

Violet had seen it too. Tess turned toward her roommate. Now that she was opening up, there was something else Tess wanted to ask her about.

"Colton led Monica by the hand into his room tonight. With Avery. Why?"

"It's her turn."

"Her turn for what?"

"To serve Colton. You've got a lot to learn for being a tier two."

Tess stared at the ceiling while she thought about what Violet had just said. "You know how Colton says the world is always against revolutionary thinkers? That we can't expect them to understand the ways of EverChange?"

"Mm hmm."

Tess ran her hand atop the down duvet. "I know we have ample security here, but does Colton ever worry about his personal safety? I mean, like all the revolutionary minds that have been killed throughout history."

"I don't know."

"We don't have any guards in the house, right? It seems like he should probably have a gun. In case any wackos managed to get inside the compound."

Violet yawned. "He does. I've seen it."

"Oh, good." Tess lay back against her pillows, trying to sound relieved. "That makes me feel better. I've never seen it on him, though."

"He doesn't carry it on him. It's in his bedside table."

"When did you see it?" Tess asked.

Violet lowered her voice. "One of the nights when it was my turn. He opened the drawer of his bedside table to get a condom. I was blindfolded but I could see through the bottom of it. There was a pistol lying next to a bunch of sex toys."

Tess's heart broke for the girl. She wondered what had happened to all these women to make them believe this was what they deserved. How their desires to improve themselves left them so vulnerable to such deceit.

"Does everyone *serve* Colton?"

Violet yawned. "Yeah. Although, from the way Avery looked at you tonight at dinner, you might not get invited for a while."

CHAPTER TWENTY-NINE

"Wake up!"

Tess ignored the distant voice and placed her hand in Colton's outstretched palm. He whispered in her ear, making her laugh as he led her toward the cliff edge of his magnificent estate. A thin layer of fog floated above the lawn in the early morning light.

They stopped at the top of the cliff and looked across the bay. Colton pulled his hand from hers and moved his palm to the small of her back. She turned toward him. She stared into his ocean blue eyes as he brought his mouth to hers.

"Tess!" the distant voice called again.

Tess pulled away and lost her balance over the side of the cliff. She reached for Colton as she fell over the edge. But instead of stretching out his hand to her, he stepped back. He flashed her a smile as Tess plummeted toward the rocky shore.

"Wake up!"

Tess opened her eyes to darkness. She pushed away the hands that gripped her shoulders and sat up in bed. A dark figure leaned over her, and it took her a moment to remember where she was.

"Tess, come on. Get up!"

She placed a hand over her chest as she recognized Violet's voice. Her heart pounded from being startled awake.

"Why? What time is it?"

"A few of us are going to give Summer a proper send off before she leaves tomorrow by doing a final trust exercise. Here, get dressed."

Tess felt her clothes land on her lap.

"I can't see."

Violet flicked on the lamp and Tess saw she was already dressed, wearing the same leggings and sweater she had tossed onto the bed. She also wore a headlamp around her forehead.

"Turn off the light when you're done and meet me in the hall. And be quiet when you come out. Colton and Avery don't know what we're doing."

"Okay." Tess felt uneasy as she got dressed. Was this a trap? Did they know the true reason she was here?

Violet was waiting right outside their door when Tess stepped into the hall.

"This way," she whispered.

Tess followed her down the dark hall until Violet stopped at the linen closet and opened the door. She crouched to the floor and turned on her head lamp. Tess silently watched her feel around on the floor until she heard a click. Violet lifted the closet floorboards in one piece.

From her headlamp, Tess could make out a ladder beneath the opening. Violet turned around and signaled Tess to stay quiet by bringing a finger to her lips. She handed Tess her own headlamp and disappeared down the stairs.

Tess looked up and down the empty hall before she followed. *Where were the others?*

The ladder creaked with each step the girls took. Tess quietly cleared her throat from the dust that lingered in the air and swiped a couple cobwebs out of her way on the way down. Tess counted over twenty steps before they reached the bottom.

"This is the old servant's passageway," Violet whispered.

Their headlamps illuminated a narrow tunnel. The opening was only an inch taller than Tess. She felt a rise of panic in her chest in the claustrophobic space. They were under the house. And she didn't like it at all.

"It leads to the pool house, which used to be a servant's quarters. It will keep us from being seen on the security cameras."

Tess worked to slow her breathing as she followed her roommate. Finally, they came to another ladder. Tess was filled with relief as she ascended the steps.

They were in the middle of the pool house when they got to the top, and Violet replaced the floorboards over the opening.

"Where's everyone else?" Tess asked when they stepped outside.

"Turn off your headlamp."

Tess complied and walked with Violet away from the castle.

"They're already there. And there's only a few of us. Summer, Aspen, Monica, and Camilla. Just a friendly competition. And a little fun."

Tess's eyes adjusted to the dark when they reached the bluff, and, with the help of the moonlight, she could make out the silhouettes of the four other women.

"Let's get started," Violet announced. "Monica, do you have the blindfolds?"

There was a confident authority in Violet's voice and Tess knew she was the instigator of this whole thing.

"Yes." Portia's roommate stepped toward Violet.

"All right. This is just like the trust exercise we did the other day. Summer, this is going to help you keep your EverChange values when you leave us tomorrow. Except, since it's night, it will be harder for your master to judge the edge of the cliff. So, this is your chance to prove your development, trust, and inner focus by tuning into your master's voice and awareness of the cliffside."

She handed Tess a blindfold. "Let's pair up. I'll be a master for the first round and tell us when to start and stop."

Tess felt a hand on her arm.

"I'll be your partner."

She recognized Summer's voice. "Okay."

"If you were given a blindfold, put it on now," Violet said. "Then, I'll say when to start."

Tess assessed the edge of the bluff before tying her blindfold behind her head. She wasn't about to go near that edge again, no matter what her *master* told her to do.

"Begin!"

Summer spoke closer to Tess's ear than Violet had when she did this the first time. But with the blindfold and three voices speaking at once, it was still disorienting.

"Take one step to the right," she heard Summer say.

"Step forward. Now back." The other masters called out their commands a few feet away.

Tess did as Summer instructed and appreciated the actress not directing her too close to the edge. At least, so far. She focused on tuning out every voice except for

Summer's. Tess trusted Summer not to lead her over the edge, but not enough to bet her life on it.

"Step forward," Summer said in Tess's ear.

"Step left!" Tess heard another voice say.

Tess took a small step forward, gradually transferring her weight once she felt a firm surface beneath her foot.

A sharp scream interrupted Summer's next command. The scream faded, sounding more and more distant, until it suddenly stopped. Tess ripped off her blindfold.

Summer ran to Violet's side at the edge of the cliff and turned on her headlamp. She leaned over the edge.

"Aspen!"

There was no answer. She turned to Violet who squinted from the light from Summer's headlamp.

"You bitch! You told her to walk off the cliff!" She shoved her with both hands before looking back over the edge and screamed her roommate's name again. There was no response.

Violet turned on her headlamp and got in Summer's face. "Don't push me! And I didn't tell her to walk off the cliff. She wasn't listening. It was an accident!"

Tess ran to the edge and turned on her lamp. But the beach was too far down to be able to see anything.

"We have to help her!" Summer turned to Tess. "We need to get down there!"

"There's no way down from here," Violet said.

"We should call 9-1-1," Tess said. But that was hard to do without a phone. "Do any of you have cell phones?"

"No," Summer said, still staring over the edge. She called her roommate's name again.

"Stop screaming," Violet said.

Summer pushed her again, this time knocking Violet to

the ground. Tess pulled Summer back from the cliff.

"Don't tell me to stop screaming! You pyscho bitch!" Summer yelled as Violet got to her feet.

"I'll go get Colton," Monica said. "He can call for help. And he'll know the quickest way to get down there."

"I'll go with you," Violet said.

Tess kept her hand on Summer's arm to keep her from lunging at Violet as she trotted past them. The others followed after them. Summer pulled her arm free from Tess's hold and ran back to the cliff.

"Hurry!" Tess called to the girls before she ran after Summer.

Summer stood dangerously close to the edge as she screamed her roommate's name. She sobbed as she waited for a response. Tess put her arm around her shaking shoulders.

"We have to help her! Maybe I can get down there. It might be her only chance."

Tess pulled her a step back from the edge. "You can't. There's no way down from here, especially in the dark. We have to wait for help to come."

Tess's mind reeled with how she could have participated in this. She should've made Summer put the blindfold on first. Maybe then she could've intervened. If Summer was right, Violet did it on purpose. She might as well have pushed her.

Tess was sick to her stomach. It was one thing to arrive at homicides after the fact, when she had nothing to do with them. It was a whole other deal to witness one, and not have had the foresight to stop it.

Summer cried against Tess's chest.

"Summer, I don't think there's much chance she

could've survived falling that far onto the rocky beach. Why don't we go join the others? They should've called 9-1-1 by now. Colton must know the quickest way to get to the beach. Maybe we can meet the medics there, or even get to her first."

"I don't want to leave her," Summer choked on her words. "What if she calls out to us?"

She won't, Tess thought. Violet had led her to her death.

She grabbed Summer's hand. "Let's go see if we can get to her."

Summer called Aspen's name a few more times before reluctantly allowing Tess to lead her back to the castle.

CHAPTER THIRTY

Tess heard women talking in the formal living room when they got inside. Summer and Tess found Violet and the two others who'd witnessed Aspen's fall sitting around the fire, along with a couple other girls who must've woken up from the commotion.

"Where's Colton and Avery? Did they call 9-1-1?" The anger was obvious in the actress's voice.

"Yes," Violet said from her spot on the couch. "They went to meet the emergency crew at the closest beach access point to here so they can show them where she fell."

"Did anyone else go with them?"

"No." Violet stared into the fireplace.

"I'm going too. I'll find the keys and take one of the SUVs."

"You can't," Violet said as Summer moved toward the door.

Summer whipped around and narrowed her eyes at the reality star. "Excuse me?"

"Colton and Avery said we have to stay here," Camilla said. "Aspen's famous. There's going to be media involvement, and they want to keep it as quiet as possible.

They want to make sure none of the facts get mixed up when talking to the authorities."

Summer scoffed. "You mean that you pushed her off the cliff?"

Violet jumped out of her seat. Tess grabbed Summer's arm as she stormed toward her.

"Stop!" Tess said.

"I'm going to help her. And I'm not going to sit here and pretend nothing happened so they can cover it up!"

Tess let go of Summer's arm when she turned for the door.

"Georgina won't let you out the front gate. She has orders from Colton and Avery not to let anyone leave until they get back."

"Georgina's really short-tempered. *I* wouldn't try and cross her when she has a loaded rifle in her hands," Camilla added.

Violet plopped back onto the couch. "There's nothing more you could do anyway. We just have to wait."

Tess and Summer exchanged a look as they decided what to do.

"This is all your fault," Summer said to Violet before taking a seat in an antique armchair.

Tess sat in one next to her and they waited mostly in silence for over an hour.

Tess checked her watch. It was after three a.m.

"This is ridiculous. They should be back by now," Summer said.

Tess had been thinking the same thing. She had a bad gut feeling that nothing was being done for the Olympic skier.

"It might've taken them awhile to find her," Violet said.

That was possible, Tess thought. But if Colton and Avery really wanted to save her, their main concern wouldn't have been covering it up.

"Isn't there a landline?" Tess asked. "Can we call them and see what's going on?"

"I don't think any of us know Colton or Avery's cell phone numbers." Violet looked around the room. "Right?"

Summer stood from her chair. "Maybe we should call 9-1-1? Make sure the search is underway?"

Although it was exactly what Tess had been thinking, she was glad, for the sake of her cover, that Summer had been the one to say it. She watched Violet's eyes narrow at the actress and a few others stiffen at Summer's words.

"Are you *questioning* Colton and Avery? Undermining their leadership? *And* the EverChange values?" Violet got up from the couch and stepped toward the actress. "Maybe it's a good thing you're leaving tomorrow. I don't think you belong here."

Summer looked ready to attack the redhead when they heard Colton and Avery come through the front door. Violet turned and stormed out of the room. Without a word, the rest of the women got up and followed her into the entry way. Avery and Colton were wet from the rain, and Tess could tell by their expressions that this wasn't going to be good.

Summer pushed to the front of the group. "Did you find her? Is she alive?"

Avery shook her head. "I'm so sorry, Summer. She must've already gotten washed out to sea."

Summer fell to her knees on the herringbone floor and wept into her hands.

Avery knelt beside her and put a hand on her back.

"There was nothing we could do."

"Emergency responders are still looking for her, right? Did they call the Coast Guard?" Tess asked.

Avery glanced up at Colton, and Tess watched them exchange a knowing look.

"We didn't see a reason to alert the media before we found her body," Colton said.

"*What?*" Summer looked up through her tears. "You never called 9-1-1?"

Avery rubbed her back. "I'm sorry, but we did everything we could."

"What does the media have to do with saving Aspen's life? We have to call 9-1-1!" Tess said.

Colton and Avery looked unmoved by what Tess had said. Summer stood and stared at them in shock. She stepped out of Avery's reach and spun around until she locked eyes with Violet.

"You *lied!* You said they called 9-1-1. That they were helping her!" Summer closed the distance between herself and the reality star. Before anyone could stop it, Summer's hands wrapped around Violet's neck.

Violet raised her arms to push Summer away, but she was overpowered by the actress's rage. Summer pushed Violet several feet back until she slammed the redhead into an antique cabinet, shattering the glass doors with the force from Violet's head. Shards of glass fell to the floor around their feet.

"You tricked us into waiting here until it was too late! You killed her!"

Violet gritted her teeth and pushed both her palms against Summer's chest with enough force to make her release her grip on the reality star's throat. Before Summer could react, Violet lifted her knee and planted her running shoe into Summer's stomach.

Summer slid backward a few feet after she hit the floor, coming to a stop next to one of the medieval knights. She stood up and withdrew a sword from the knight's hand. Summer lifted it in the air as Violet charged her.

"Enough!" Colton yelled.

Both women paused as Colton crossed the room and stood in between them. He raised his hand toward the sword.

"Put it down, Summer."

She glared at Violet as she lowered the weapon.

Several more women wearing silk nightgowns filed into the entry way. They looked confused by all that was happening, having slept through everything until now.

Avery came and stood next to Colton. "Violet didn't lie. She thought we already called 9-1-1 before we left. We decided it would be best for everyone if we waited to make the call after we knew if there was any chance of saving her. She's an Olympic athlete, and her death would spark an investigation into all of us. And EverChange. We were protecting Aspen too. The media would undoubtedly make it seem like she was involved in something bad here. We already get accused of being a cult." Avery took a deep breath and turned to Violet. "Her death was an accident, but it would've been avoided if you hadn't been so reckless. You had no right to do what you did, and it cost Aspen her life."

"There will be other retributions," Colton added. "But for now I want you to return your necklace and bracelet. You are no longer a tier three but a tier one. And, Summer, we ask that after you go, you don't say a word of this to anyone. To protect all of our reputations, especially

Aspen's."

"Summer?" Avery asked. "Can we trust you?"

Summer held the sword at her side and nodded. "Yes, you can trust me."

Tess couldn't believe her response. Colton and Avery lied, did nothing to help Aspen, and left her to die. *But since they said it's to save their reputation, Summer's okay with it?* It made Tess wonder what Summer had been made to give up as collateral. *How could she be so blind?*

But they all were, Tess thought as she looked around the room. It was ingrained in them to trust, not question, until over time, they eventually believed whatever Colton said.

"Good. Thank you, Summer. And Violet, give your jewelry to Avery before you go upstairs. We'll continue our search for Aspen once it's light out."

Violet didn't say a word to Tess when she crept into their room, but Tess could tell from her audible sniffles that she was crying. Tess sat on their bed in the dark waiting for the first morning light to filter in through the curtains.

The reality star sat in a chair by the fireplace and began to weep. Tess flicked on the lamp and crossed the room to take a seat in the chair next to her roommate. Violet's body shook from her sobs, and she buried her face in her hands.

"I didn't mean for anyone to die. I know I might seem like I don't have a heart, but I'd never kill anyone." Violet's face was red when she looked up at Tess. "She just...slipped."

Tess wasn't sure whether to believe her. She wanted to give Violet the benefit of the doubt, since Tess had been blindfolded when it happened. But Summer was convinced

Violet led the Olympian to her death on purpose.

"I can't believe Colton is stripping me of my tier level. It was an accident!" Violet wiped her face with the back of her hand. "I'm more committed to EverChange than anyone. Why can't they see that?"

Tess realized that Violet's tears weren't for the woman who'd fallen to her death. They were because she'd lost the thing that mattered to her the most: her EverChange status. Being rebuked by Colton and Avery, her masters, had wounded her deeply.

"I've given my life to this organization," Violet continued.

Tess figured there would be no better time to press the reality star about Portia. Her bitterness toward her leaders might cause her to open up to Tess. Especially if she felt she had an ally.

Tess put her hand on Violet's shoulder. "I know."

"You believe me?"

Tess nodded. "I think they're worried about how this might reflect on EverChange and they're looking for someone to blame. I can help you talk to them once everything calms down. If you want."

Violet reached for Tess's hand on her shoulder and squeezed. "Thank you."

"Of course."

Tess let a few minutes go by before she changed the subject.

"Does it seem weird to you that no one has seen Portia since Saturday? That she didn't even come downstairs during that fight, like everyone else? I haven't told anyone this, but I went to check on her yesterday and she wasn't in her room. Monica said she was in the bathroom, but I checked all the ones upstairs. I think she lied. I'm worried about her."

Violet stared at the woven rug. "There's only a few of us who are supposed to know. But I guess I'm not one of them anymore."

"Know what, Violet?"

"She's not sick. She's in the cell."

Tess swallowed. "What's the cell?"

Violet turned in her chair to face Tess. "You have to promise not to say anything. To anyone. I'm not supposed to tell you this."

"I promise."

"It's a small house on the property where girls get sent sometimes to realign their thought patterns with those of EverChange. It's just a place of solitude where they can refocus their minds. Tier threes take turns guarding it, just like the front gate. Sometimes girls are sent there for a long time. So, it's not somewhere you want to go."

"Have you ever been to the cell?"

"No way."

"Well, then how do you—"

"Stop. No more questions. It's where my old roommate is. I've been waiting for her to come back for nearly a week. But, since they're making me room with you now, she must not be coming back." Her voice broke, and tears streamed down her face again.

"I'm sorry," Tess whispered. "What's her name?" But Tess feared she already knew the answer. And if she was right, did that mean Portia was already dead?

Violet cleared her throat.

"Her name is Andrea."

CHAPTER THIRTY-ONE

"How many girls have gone to the cell in the nine months you've been here?" Tess asked.

The first hint of daylight was filtering into their room around the velvet curtains.

Violet leaned back in her chair and absent-mindedly chewed a nail. "Four, I think. Including Portia."

"And have any of them ever come back?"

"Just one. Sophia. She was only there for a couple days."

"And how long has the other girl been there, besides Andrea and Portia?"

"Probably about five or six weeks. I'm not sure. I guess it just depends on how long it takes for them to readjust their way of thinking."

Tess leaned forward, resting her elbows on her thighs. "Have you seen the cell? Do you know where it is?"

"We're not supposed to talk about it. I've already told you too much."

"I won't tell anyone. I just want to learn how things are done here. Especially after last night."

Violet exhaled. "Sophia said it's by the airplane hangar. Behind it I think. But that's all I know. I hadn't gotten a chance to guard it yet."

"Did Sophia see the other girls when she was there?"

"I don't know. I don't think so. You're kept in solitude if you get sent there. And you're not allowed to speak of it when you come back."

"Right."

"If you really want to know how things are done here, there's something else I should tell you. We don't just serve Colton. There are others."

Tess could see that Violet was starting to enjoy this. "What do you mean?"

"Well, sometimes Colton has guests visit. Wealthy and influential men who are thinking of joining EverChange. Colton offers the um...*service* of some of the girls while these men stay. It's part of our duty in helping them find their path to enlightenment...."

Tess was deep in thought when she heard Violet's breathing change to a light snore. She turned to see the reality star crashed out in her chair. Tess got to her feet and paced in front of the fireplace before deciding to join the others to look for Aspen.

The Intel Unit had been right about the sex trafficking. And if Andrea had been killed the night the girls were told she'd been taken to the cell, Tess surmised the one who'd been there for weeks was likely dead too. She'd have to find out if it was the governor's daughter.

But what about Portia? This was the fifth day she'd been gone. Tess needed to get to the cell. Although, how could she help the girls without having a way of escape?

If what Violet said was true, the girls were not only being regularly sex-trafficked by Colton, but they were also regularly being killed. Colton had a lot to hide. There was no telling what resources he could afford to keep this quiet.

CHAPTER THIRTY-TWO

Tess stood next to Summer on the edge of the bluff. She tucked a strand of hair behind her ear that blew across her face from the wind.

"Are you still leaving today?"

Summer nodded. "I have to fly back tonight. We start filming tomorrow."

Tess gazed across the Sound to the mainland. She was surprised Colton and Avery were allowing Summer to leave after she'd been so furious over her roommate's fall. Tess feared they might be planning to take Summer to the cell. Or worse.

Colton and Avery hadn't allowed anyone off the premises to look for Aspen. After the sun came up, everyone gathered at the edge of the bluff to search for a sign of the Olympian's body. Colton said they couldn't afford to be seen on the beach and that the bluffs on the castle grounds offered a better vantage point anyway. Tess agreed about the latter; you could see the beach for miles from where they stood. But there'd been no sight of Aspen.

Colton promised to file a missing persons report, which seemed to appease most of the women. He also instructed everyone, in order to protect EverChange, to say that Aspen was suicidal if they were questioned by police.

Everyone else had already given up and gone inside to get ready for dinner.

"How are you getting to the airport?" Tess asked.

"Avery's taking me to Boeing Field in the helicopter. I'll have a private plane waiting for me there."

"Well, I want to see you off." Tess wanted to see Summer take off in the helicopter with her own eyes.

"Doesn't Colton have to go? Who's going to fly it?"

Summer shook her head. "Avery will. She has a helicopter license, too."

Tess turned to face the movie star. "It still won't be too late to tell the authorities what happened to Aspen when you get back to L.A. You could even go to the police tonight after you get to Seattle. Fly back in the morning instead."

Summer looked at Tess like she was crazy. "I can't do that. You heard what Colton said. It could ruin my career. It's too late. She's already gone. If I go to the police tonight, twenty-four hours after she fell...I'll just look guilty. Implicated. Negligent. I can't go to jail for manslaughter. And think of EverChange."

Tess wondered again what Summer gave up as collateral to move up to tier two. And if that was her motive for protecting EverChange.

"A murder investigation could bring down the whole organization," Summer went on. "I can't do that to Colton. It wasn't his fault. And Aspen wouldn't have wanted that either."

Tess was starting to see why Colton would allow Summer to go. Plus, the disappearance of an Oscar-winning actress with known connections to EverChange might spark more questions than some of their less famous members.

"I guess you're right," Tess lied.

"We better head in. It's almost time for dinner."

"What time is Avery taking you?"

"Not until nine. She's spending the night at Rachelle Morale's house on Lake Washington after she drops me off. She's been mentoring her lately."

Tess linked her arm through Summer's as they huddled together against the wind and made their way across the landscaped grounds. *Nine.* She hoped that would give her enough time to carry out her plan.

Violet looked her up and down when Tess got back to their room. "You better get ready. Colton doesn't like us being late for dinner. He sees it as a sign of disrespect."

Violet's four-inch heels clicked against the herringbone wood floor as she crossed the room.

"I'll be down in a minute." Tess reached for the sequin minidress that had been laid out atop their bed.

Violet reached for the door handle. "Hurry. I'll see you downstairs."

Tess threw her sweater onto the bed before she grabbed the designer dress and carefully unzipped it. After taking the white Christian Louboutins out of their box, she moved to the door. She paused and leaned her head against it until she recognized Colton and Avery's voices coming down the hall.

She waited a minute after their voices faded before she opened the door to her room and tiptoed into the empty hall. She moved swiftly past several doors until she came to Colton and Avery's room at the end of the hall. She paused before her hand gripped the brass handle of the double doors.

She checked behind her, making sure she was still alone. She tried the door handle, but it was locked. *How untrusting of you, Colton.* Tess glanced at the ceiling as she pulled a bobby pin out of her hair. She hadn't seen any cameras inside the castle, but that didn't mean they weren't there.

She used her teeth to open the bobby pin before sliding it into the lock. It took her less than a minute of maneuvering before she heard a click. The handle turned with ease. She withdrew the bobby pin and stepped inside the room, closing the door softly behind her.

Tess flicked on the lights and looked around the large bedroom suite. She decided to check the beside tables first but paused when she passed a wide screen computer monitor atop a small desk. Next to the computer was a small black phone that was plugged into a landline on the wall. She had no doubt it was bugged.

The computer's screen was off. Colton probably used it to view the property's security cameras. There might be some at the cell. She wiggled the mouse and the screen lit up requesting a password. She typed in *EverChange*.

Incorrect password. She bit her lip and stared at the screen. She didn't have time to try again. Not if she wanted to find a gun before dinner. She turned off the screen and went straight to the closest bedside table. She opened the top drawer to find a paperback novel set in Seattle, chapstick, and a blindfold. But no gun.

She hurried to the nightstand on the other side of the bed. She flung open the top drawer, knowing she didn't have much time. When Colton and Avery realized she wasn't at dinner, they would send someone up to get her.

Or come themselves.

The contents of the drawer slid to the front when it came to a stop. This was the drawer Violet had seen. Condoms, lube, more blindfolds, and various sex toys. Tess brushed the pile of blindfolds aside, exposing a gray 9mm SIG Sauer Semi-Auto.

When she lifted the pistol, Tess could tell from its weight that it was loaded. She moved her thumb along the side to check how many bullets she had, but the magazine release wasn't there. She turned the gun in her hand and found the release on the other side. It was made for someone left-handed.

She ejected the magazine, which was fully loaded, and slid it back into the gun before closing the drawer. She gripped the gun comfortably in her right hand, thankful for Colton's good taste in firearms. His SIG Sauer was a new model, equipped with high-visibility day and night sights.

Tess locked their door from the inside before flicking off the lights and pulling it closed. She turned the handle, making sure it was locked before she dashed down the hall.

She shut the door behind her when she got to her room and looked for a good place to stash the gun while she went down for dinner. There was a knock on her door. She spun around, gun in hand.

"Tess?"

It was Avery.

"Are you okay?"

Tess ran to her bed and slid the gun under her pillow as Avery opened the door. Tess leaned against the bed and slipped her feet into her Christian Louboutins.

"Sorry," Tess said. "I was having trouble with the zipper on my dress."

Avery came toward her. "Do you need some help?"

Tess stepped into her second heel and stood. She prayed she'd completely covered the gun in her rush, but she didn't dare turn around to check.

"I got it. Thank you." She moved toward the door, feeling her heart beat against her chest. "I guess I'm just not used to these nice clothes."

Avery smiled. "Trust me, once you get used to them, you'll never want to go back. And, as long as you're here with us, you won't need to."

Tess let out a sigh of relief when Avery followed her out the door. Tess pulled the door shut behind her and allowed Avery to lead the way down the stairs.

"I hope you're hungry," Avery said.

"Starving." That, at least, she didn't have to lie about.

"The girls have prepared one of my favorite dinners tonight: grilled octopus. You're going to love it."

"Was Colton able to file a missing persons report for Aspen today?"

Avery paused on the steps and turned around to face Tess. "Not yet. But I'm sure he'll do it first thing tomorrow. We're both distraught over what happened."

Avery continued down the stairs, and Tess followed.

Not distraught enough to do anything to save her, she thought.

Tess and Violet got back to their room at the same time after dinner. Tess had felt Colton's eyes on her for almost the entire dinner. She wasn't sure if he was coming on to her or suspicious of her. She'd refused to meet his gaze and instead worked out her plan for the evening while she made small talk with the girl next to her. Colton concluded the dinner with a toast in honor of Aspen. Tess felt sickened by his words, knowing there was blood on his hands for covering up her death.

As soon as Violet pulled her dress over her head, Tess reached for the SIG Sauer under her pillow. She closed her fingers around the grip and held it behind her back as Violet grabbed her nightgown off the bed. Tess watched Violet pull on her nightgown as she slid the gun barrel under her bra strap beneath the back of the sequin dress for lack of a better place to hide the firearm. The dress was just tight enough for the gun to fit without falling down her back.

"You going to wear that to bed?" Violet asked.

Tess pushed her long, blonde hair behind both shoulders to cover the pistol grip that was still exposed. "Actually, I'm gonna go say good-bye to Summer. Avery is flying her to the airport in an hour."

"Oh. I thought you said good-bye to her earlier."

"Sort of. But it's been a tough twenty-four hours. I just want to make sure she leaves on a positive note."

"Good idea. I might be asleep when you get back. I'm exhausted."

Violet didn't seem to lose any sleep over her role in Aspen's death. "Good night," Tess said before opening their door.

"Good night."

Tess made sure the hall was empty before she stepped out of their room. She glanced at Colton and Avery's closed door at the end of the hall. She slipped off her heels and carried them in one hand as she made her way to the linen closet Violet had led her through last night.

After opening the closet door, she crouched down and felt for the handle. Her fingers closed around it and she lifted the baseboards. She climbed down the ladder, pausing to close the closet door after a few steps.

The cement was cold and damp on her bare feet when she reached the floor of the passageway. She slipped on her heels and ducked to fit through the narrow tunnel. It was pitch-black without the light from a headlamp. Tess ran her hand against the cobweb-covered wall to find her way to the other side of the passageway.

When she stepped out the back door of the pool house, she triggered a motion-sensor light. She'd seen a deer trigger the lights earlier that week and hoped it would go unnoticed as she moved to the edge of the building. She waited for the light to turn off before she cut across the side lawn. Her eyes were still adjusting to the dark when she got to the wooded area. She tripped over a tree branch and her momentum sent her crashing to the ground. She reached behind and made sure the gun was still held by her dress before getting up.

She brushed her hands against her sequin dress as she continued through the woods, stepping as quietly and quickly as she could in the dark forest. She paused every few feet to ensure she wasn't being followed. When she reached the clearing, she pulled the gun from her dress.

She could make out the airstrip and hangar in the distance from the sliver of moonlight that peeked through the clouds. She scanned the field before she broke into a run. Her platform heels clacked against the asphalt runway when she crossed the airstrip then quieted again as she took long strides over the wet grass. She'd surprised herself by how well she could run in four-inch heels.

Tess slowed when she reached the hangar. Her fingers gripped the pistol in her right hand as she crept alongside the pole building. When she reached the back of the hangar, another white pole building came into view, half the size of the hangar. She knew it had to be the cell.

When she got closer, Tess spotted Monica, the retired tennis pro, sitting in a chair at the front of the smaller building. A shotgun was propped against her side as she read a book under the building's outdoor light.

Tess pressed her back against the hangar and slipped off her heels. She moved away from the building, making a wide berth before she ran straight for the tennis player's back with her gun outstretched. She came to a stop with her gun inches from the back of Monica's head.

Her head remained down, focused on a novel. She wore the same radio on her shoulder that Tess had seen on the celebrity chef when she escorted Tess back to the castle from her walk. Tess swiped the shotgun off the ground as she thrust the barrel of the pistol into the base of Monica's skull.

"Put your hands on your head."

The tennis pro's body jerked and her book fell to ground. She started to turn around, but Tess pressed the gun harder into her neck.

"I *said* put your hands on your head."

Slowly, the athlete did as she was told. "I knew it was a mistake for Colton to bring you here. He should've never trusted a cop."

"Get up and unlock the door."

But instead of getting to her feet, Monica's hand went for her radio. "I need—"

Tess slammed the pistol into her temple. Monica groaned as her hand released the radio and held the side of her face. Tess thrust the barrel beneath the woman's jaw and pressed upward toward her mouth.

"*Ahhh!*" Monica leaned to the side, trying to ease the pressure from the gun to her throat.

A crackled voice came through her radio. "Everything okay?"

Tess set the shotgun on the ground behind her and lifted her hand to the radio. "Tell her everything is fine."

She pressed the *talk* button and let up slightly on the pistol's pressure to Monica's throat.

"Yeah, everything's fine," she said through gritted teeth.

"Did you need something?" the crackled voice replied.

"Tell her no." Tess pressed the *talk* button again.

Monica cleared her throat. "No. Sorry, nevermind."

"Okay."

Tess ripped the radio from Monica's shirt and threw it into the field beside the building. She withdrew the gun from the tennis pro's neck and moved around in front of her, keeping the gun aimed on her chest.

"Stand up slowly with your hands on your head."

Monica stood to her feet. Tess inched toward her and motioned for the door with her gun.

"Open it."

She walked to the door. "You don't want to do this. Colton will never forgive you."

"Just do it."

Tess kept the pistol fixed on Monica as she reached for the keys hanging from her hip. After she had unlocked the door, Tess pressed the end of the gun into the champion's back and followed her inside.

The cement-floored hallway was lined with two doors on each side. *How many girls are they keeping here?* All the doors locked from the outside with both a deadbolt and turnkey lock.

Tess motioned for the first door on the right. "Open this one first."

After she turned the deadlock, Monica slid one of the keys into the lock. The door opened to an empty room. The small, windowless room looked just like a prison. There was a cot against the wall and a toilet and small sink in the corner.

Tess ripped the keys from Monica's hand and gave her back a shove. She closed the heavy door and flipped the deadlock, leaving the tennis pro in the cell. Tess tried a few of the keys before one fit into the turnkey lock.

Monica banged against the door. "You can't do this! This is for the girls' own good! Colton will be furious when he finds out!"

Although Tess could tell she was yelling, Monica's voice was muted. Tess wondered if the rooms were soundproofed as she unlocked the next door. It looked identical to the room she'd locked Monica in. Also empty.

She hurried to the next one. She didn't have much time before Avery left with Summer.

Tess swung open the door and found Portia crouched in the corner of the cell. She looked up at Tess with terrified eyes. She wore the same leggings and sweater as she had last Saturday, but she was otherwise almost unrecognizable. Her platinum blonde hair was a matted mess and there were pronounced dark circles under her eyes.

"Portia! It's okay. I'm here to help you."

Portia remained hunched in the corner.

"We need to go. *Now.*"

Portia stared at the gun in Tess's hand as she motioned toward the door.

"I don't deserve to leave yet."

Her words took Tess by surprise. "Yes, you do. Portia, I need you to trust me. You don't belong in here."

Portia wrapped her arms around her legs. Her eyes were filled with fear as she fixed her gaze on the open doorway.

Portia probably thought this was some kind of test and she'd be punished for leaving.

"I'm a detective, and I came to get you out. But we don't have much time. Is there anyone else here?

"Portia?"

The girl met Tess's gaze. "Umm...yes. There's one more girl. In the room next to me. She talks to me sometimes."

"Okay. Let's go."

Portia slowly got to her feet as Tess ran to the next room. She tried two keys before one slid into the lock. She opened the door and saw Portia was right. An emaciated brunette looked up at Tess and Portia from her cot. Her appearance was even more disheveled than Portia. She looked like she'd been starved for a long time.

The girl's tired eyes moved from Tess to Portia. Tess moved toward her. When she looked into the girl's green eyes, she recognized her. She looked completely different than the smiling, healthy girl Tess had seen in the Intel Unit's photos, but the eyes were the same.

"Charity, it's time to go," Tess said. "I'm here to get you out of here."

"Back to the castle?" The girl's voice was weak.

Tess shook her head. "No. Away from this place. Free."

The girl looked confused. "Does Colton know you're here?"

"No."

Tess helped her sit up in bed. She'd never seen anyone

so thin. Her hand completely closed around Charity's upper arm when Tess pulled her to a seated position. The governor's daughter was going to die if she didn't get help soon.

"Oh my—Charity!" Portia rushed to her side and wrapped her arms around the frail girl.

"Can you stand?" Tess asked.

"Um. I don't know."

Tess and Portia helped Charity to her feet. But Tess realized Charity barely had the strength to speak, let alone walk. Her knees buckled as soon as she stood, and she fell back onto the cot.

Portia looked desperately at Tess. "She's too weak."

Tess quickly considered their options. Even if she carried Charity to the helicopter, Charity wouldn't have the strength to escape once they got to Seattle. Tess thought about taking her chances with the guard at the front gate. But even if Tess shot her way out, she wouldn't get far without a car or a phone. And Colton would have plenty of time to kill Charity or take her somewhere else before she got back with reinforcements.

They would have to leave her. For now. Tess ran out the front door of the cell and grabbed the tennis player's water bottle off the ground. Tess remembered seeing it by the chair next to a small brown sack. She tore open the paper bag and pulled out an apple and a protein bar.

When Tess got back to Charity's cell, she opened the protein bar and handed her the food and water.

"I'll be right back," Tess said, as Charity took a drink.

Tess returned with Monica's shotgun less than a minute later. She leaned it against the side of her cot. "Use this if Colton or one of the women tries to hurt you before I get back."

Charity looked with wide eyes at the gun. Suddenly, she lunged for the weapon. Her hands weakly grasped the barrel before Tess pulled it out of her hands.

"You can't do this!" Charity fell onto her cot. "If Colton finds out, he'll punish all of us!"

Tess put a hand on the frail girl's shoulders. *Couldn't Charity see that's what was already happening?* "Charity, you're going to die if we don't get you out of here. I need to send for help. Do you understand? We should have you out by the morning."

Charity looked to be processing what Tess had said as she took a bite of the protein bar.

"I need you to stay here for a little longer. Can you do that?"

She nodded. "Okay."

"Come on." Tess grabbed Portia by the arm. "Let's go."

Tess pumped the shotgun and leaned it against Charity's cell wall. Charity had already lain down on her cot when Tess turned. "If you need to use this, all you have to do is pull the trigger."

Tess walked backward to the front of the building, making sure Charity didn't get a second wind and come at them with the shotgun. Once she and Portia were outside, Tess locked the door behind them. Monica's cries for help were barely audible from outside the building.

Tess turned to Portia. "I'm going to try and get you off the island tonight. But you have to do everything I say."

Portia nodded.

"We're going to cross the field, go through the wooded area, then cross the back of the house to the helicopter pad. Stay close to me and don't speak. And when we get behind the house, you need to be far enough away not to set off any motion-sensor lights or be seen in the surveillance cameras. If we get separated, I want you to meet me at the helicopter."

"Okay."

"Do you think you can run?" Tess asked.

"I think so."

"Let's go."

Tess gripped Colton's gun in her right hand as she led Portia in a jog across the airfield. She slowed her pace slightly so Portia could keep up while she scanned the area to make sure they weren't spotted.

Portia fell twice inside the wooded area but returned to her feet with Tess's help. Tess held her arm out for Portia to stop when they reached the clearing behind the castle.

The helipad was lit, and Tess was filled with relief to see the chopper was still there. Tess led Portia across the lawn, moving as quickly as she could without losing her. Tess looked around when they reached the empty helicopter. They seemed to be alone on the grounds. She eased open the door, sliding it as quietly as possible, and turned to the young woman.

"Climb into the back. Behind the seats. And stay low. Avery is taking Summer to Boeing Field tonight. You can't trust either of them. Wait until they're not looking and get away from them as quickly as possible. Once you get away, use someone's phone or have them take you to the Seattle Police Headquarters downtown. Ask for Homicide Detective Blake Stephenson. Tell him Tess sent you and that they need to come to the compound *now*; we can't wait until next week."

"Wait, you're not coming with me?"

Tess shook her head. "I can't. If Violet alerts Colton that I'm missing, and he checks the cell, he might kill Charity."

"Okay." Portia climbed inside and crawled over the back seats.

Tess handed her Colton's gun. "Take this. Just in case."

Portia reluctantly accepted the pistol.

"It's ready to fire. If you need it, click this safety off and then all you have to do is pull the trigger. Stay low and don't make a sound. Remember, Homicide Detective Blake Stephenson."

Tess looked around before she slid the helicopter door closed and walked back toward the house. She went in through the door to the butler's pantry, even though it meant she set off the light. That was better than being seen on a surveillance camera. She slipped off her stilettos and crept through the quiet mansion.

She passed the medieval knights and came face-to-face with Avery and Summer when she started up the stairs. They'd both changed out of their evening dresses and each held a Louis Vuitton suitcase in their hands.

"I stopped by your room," Summer said. "But Violet said you'd left to say good-bye to me."

Tess smiled. "Yeah, I thought you'd already gone down to the helicopter. I'm glad I didn't miss you."

Summer eyed the heels Tess carried in her hand.

Tess smiled. "And I guess I'm not used to these heels. You want help with your bags?"

"We're good," Avery said.

"I'll walk out with you," Tess said, following them through the formal living area.

"I'm going to miss you," Summer said to Tess as they stepped outside.

"What sort of movie are you filming?"

"It's this twisty thriller about a guy who gets an organ transplant from a serial killer. Remember what I said about paying me a visit."

"I will." When they neared the helipad, Tess was glad to see the helicopter door was still shut and Portia couldn't be seen through the outside windows.

Tess and Summer hugged good-bye as Avery slid open the door. She looked over Summer's shoulder and watched Avery lift Summer's bags into the back seats. Portia was hiding right behind them.

Tess exhaled when Avery turned around and went to the pilot's seat to start up the helicopter.

"I hope you find your inner strength here," Summer said before climbing in next to Avery. "Like I did."

Tess made a conscious effort to avert her eyes from the backseat. "I'm sure I will. Have a good trip back."

Tess's hair blew from the wind created by the spinning rotor blades as she watched the helicopter lift off. She watched the chopper soar over the edge of the bluff and prayed Portia would keep her wits about her to stay undetected for the rest of the trip.

The lights were off in her room when Tess opened the door.

"I left your nightgown on the bed," Violet said.

"Thanks."

When Tess climbed into their bed, she looked over at her roommate's silhouette. She lay awake, hoping she'd done the right thing by putting Portia on the helicopter. She knew it was a risk. If Colton found out Portia escaped, he'd try to have her killed. But Tess couldn't leave them both locked in the cell. Charity might not live until Tess's check-in next week.

Quiet sobs erupted from the pillow next to her. She'd thought Violet was asleep. Tess turned her head toward her roommate.

"What's wrong?"

Violet's voice came out a whisper. "It's my fault Andrea got sent to the cell."

Tess propped herself up with her elbow. "What do you mean?"

"I caught her sneaking out of our room one night. She said she was just going to the bathroom, but when she didn't come back for a while I went to check on her. She wasn't there."

She let out a loud sniff.

"I told on her. I didn't know where she went, just that it was against the rules to leave without permission after lights out. A few days later, I learned she'd been sent to the cell."

"What happened to Andrea isn't your fault. You thought you were doing the right thing by telling Colton."

"No, not Colton. He was already asleep."

"Then who'd you tell?"

Violet fell silent.

"Avery?"

For a moment, Tess thought she wasn't going to answer. When Violet finally spoke, her voice was so quiet Tess could barely hear her.

"Yes."

CHAPTER THIRTY-THREE

Portia leaned her head forward against the back seat of the helicopter. Summer and Avery's voices were drowned out by the hum of the motor and whir from the rotor blades as the small chopper lifted off from the ground. She rested the pistol against her leg and tried not to cry.

She'd never been so scared in her life. She didn't really know Tess, and now she worried that she'd been wrong to trust her. She said she was a detective. So, she'd only been at the castle to spy on them?

Portia hadn't liked being in the cell. But in the days she'd been there, she realized she'd been wrong to question EverChange. She was just so upset when she'd nearly fallen off the cliff. At first, she'd thought it was intentional. That Monica had been trying to kill her. But what if she really had just misheard her roommate's instruction?

There were so many people talking at once during the exercise. Maybe Colton and Avery were right. It was an accident. And maybe even her own fault for not being tuned in enough to her master.

Portia lifted her head above the seat. The lights from the control panel illuminated the small fuselage with a soft glow.

Avery said something to Summer that Portia couldn't make out. Summer pulled off her headset and whipped around in her seat, feeling around the rear seats with her hand. Portia ducked her head below the seat backs.

"I can't find it," she heard Summer yell.

Maybe she should just tell Avery the truth. She didn't want to get in any more trouble with her, and Colton. And they had been so good to her. EverChange had in fact changed her life.

She peeked over the seat back again to see Summer completely turned around on her knees, reaching behind her seat as if she were looking for something on the floor.

Portia was sure they were going to let her out of the cell any day. They were only giving her time to align her thinking. It was for her own good. They loved her. She felt a wash guilt for this attempt to run away.

And Charity must have done something very bad to be kept in the cell so long. It had to be her own fault, or maybe something to do with her mother. It was no secret the state governor despised Charity's involvement with EverChange. Colton would only be keeping her there to help her. Because he loved her, too.

She was about to speak up when Avery leaned over and pulled open the door on Summer's side of the cockpit. They were instantly accosted by a cold, fierce wind that filled the small aircraft.

Portia sat all the way up. The helicopter banked to the left and she fell against the side wall. She gripped the seat back and pulled herself up. She watched Summer's eyes widen as her body leaned toward the open door and she frantically felt for something to hang on to.

"What are you doing?" Summer screamed. "I don't have

my seatbelt on!" Her fingers gripped the back of her seat.

Suddenly the aircraft dipped again. Portia watched in horror as Avery gave Summer's side a shove and the movie star disappeared out the open door.

"Summer!" Portia screamed. She reached her arm out for the actress, but it was too late.

Avery leveled the helicopter and whipped around. Her eyes met Portia's. Portia's mouth hung open in shock. She realized Tess had been right.

"Portia?"

A chill that was not from the wind ran down Portia's back. She tightened her grip on the pistol.

Avery's eyes narrowed. "What the hell are you doing back there?"

CHAPTER THIRTY-FOUR

Three weeks. How could they expect Tess to stay at that cult compound for that long?

Stephenson rolled over and checked the time on his phone. Nearly midnight.

After his conversation with Wallace, he'd gone to see Lieutenant Greyson, who, instead of hearing his concerns for Tess, all but threatened Stephenson's job if he didn't back off.

He had to do something. She couldn't stay there for three weeks. Women had been killed because of their connection to EverChange. If Colton suspected what she was really doing there....

He couldn't allow himself to think about it. He needed enough proof to convince a judge to sign off on a warrant for the Whidbey compound. But since his hands were tied by the department in pursuing Everett for Andrea's murder, that wasn't going to be easy. Even Avery's phone records, or the fact that Colton and Parker didn't have a prenup, weren't enough to prove he killed her.

Stephenson sat up in bed and rubbed the side of his face. He might as well work if he wasn't going to sleep. He got up and went to get his laptop when his phone rang. He wasn't on call. Seeing the number for Police Headquarters, he answered.

"Detective Stephenson."

"Hi, Detective. This is Officer Chen. I'm sorry to call at this time of night, but we've had a woman come in who says she needs to speak to you, and it can't wait."

Tess. He flicked on the light.

"She says a detective named Tess helped her escape a place on Whidbey Island where she was imprisoned and told her to find you. Her story sounds pretty out there, but she says that another woman was murdered during her escape."

"Thanks for calling. I'm coming now. Can you stay with her until I get there? Did she say anything else?"

Blake put the call on speaker while he pulled on his pants.

"Just that her name's Portia Grenalli."

CHAPTER THIRTY-FIVE

Officer Chen was waiting for him when the elevator doors opened to the seventh floor. Stephenson followed him down the hall of the Homicide Unit. He'd worried about Tess the entire drive. *Why hadn't she gone with the girls she'd helped escape? And, if one of the girls had been killed, did that mean Tess had been found out?*

"I brought her up here and gave her a sandwich." He motioned to the small room on his left that they referred to as the soft room. It was similar to their interview rooms, but it was carpeted and included cushioned chairs that weren't bolted to the floor.

"She said she's hardly eaten in a few days."

"Okay. Thank you."

"Sure." He pushed the door open. "Portia, this is Detective Blake Stephenson."

A beautiful woman with a mess of blonde hair looked up. There were dark smudges of mascara under both her eyes. An empty sandwich wrapper lay on her lap.

"Hi." Stephenson held out his hand.

She accepted his hand with a weak grip. Stephenson sat down across from her.

"Are you hurt?"

She shook her head. "I feel a little better now that I've had some food."

He was dying to ask her if Tess was okay. "Would you mind if we spoke in one of our interview rooms? That way, I can record our conversation, if that's okay with you."

The officer nodded to Stephenson before disappearing down the empty hall. Her green eyes met his. Stephenson recognized a look of fear take over her face.

"Um. Could we talk here first?"

He needed her to feel comfortable enough to speak freely. "Sure. But I'll probably need you to make a formal statement at some point."

She nodded. "Okay."

"Can you state your full name for me?"

"Portia Granelli."

There was something familiar about her, but he couldn't quite place it. "And can you tell me what happened tonight? And why you came here?"

Tears brimmed from her eyes as they met his.

"I've been staying at the EverChange mansion on Whidbey Island for the last six months. We call it the castle. Things had been going okay, until a few days ago when I was taken to the cell."

"What kind of cell?"

"A locked room with no window. No toilet other than a bucket. It was a prison. There was a sink for water, but I hadn't had any food for a few days."

Her hand trembled as she tucked a tangled strand of hair behind her ear.

"And how did you get out?"

"Tess."

Hearing her name, his heart quickened.

"She rescued me. Helped me hide in the back of Colton's helicopter. She gave me a gun and told me to find you after we landed." Her lower lip quivered, and she dropped her gaze to the table.

"You told Officer Chen that there was another woman who was murdered during your escape. Can you tell me what happened?"

She nodded, but it took her a moment before she could speak. A tear ran down the side of her face.

"We'd just taken off from the castle. I was hiding behind the backseats of the helicopter, and I was starting to have second thoughts about escaping. I mean, EverChange was my life, and it's helped me a lot.

"Summer was in the front seat next to Colton. When I sat up, she was turned around looking for something in the backseat. She had her seat belt off. Colton opened the door on her side. And, um...." She rubbed her fingers against her forehead. "He pushed her. He pushed her out the door."

"And you said you'd just taken off when this happened?"

"We'd been flying for maybe ten minutes, I'd guess. It was dark, but it looked like we were over water."

"Okay. I'm going to get a search and rescue team in place to look for Summer. Do you know her last name? And can you tell me what she looked like?"

"Channing. Summer Channing. You know, the actress? She just won an Oscar."

"I do." While he knew there were some celebrities affiliated with EverChange, he was surprised someone so famous had been at Colton's Whidbey Island estate. "And so how did you escape?"

"I still had the gun Tess had given me after Colton

pushed Summer out of the helicopter. I pointed it at him, but I knew I couldn't use it. Not if I wanted to live. He tried to convince me it had been an accident. That she fell when the chopper dipped to the side. I pretended to believe him.

"When we landed, I made him open the door. But after he opened it, he knocked the gun out of my hands. It hit the tarmac and skidded behind him. I knew there was no way I could overpower him without the gun, so I just jumped out and ran.

"He was supposed to take Summer to Boeing Field. I'm not totally sure, but I think that's where we landed. I ran across a tarmac, past some hangars, and over a railroad track. He chased me, and I ended up in a forested area after going under the freeway." She stared at Stephenson's hands atop the table. "The gun went off twice, but he missed. I hid for probably an hour while he searched the woods for me. Finally, I couldn't hear him anymore. After I heard a helicopter take off, I ran through the woods until I came to a neighborhood. An older couple answered their door and brought me here."

Tears spilled out of her eyes as she met his gaze. "Colton's evil. He's a master manipulator. Please, you have to arrest him and save the other women at the castle."

Like Tess, he thought. "Could you tell if it was Colton's helicopter that you saw take off?"

She stared at the floor before answering. "Not for sure, but I think so."

"I'll see if I can get Boeing Field's air traffic control to ground all helicopters until we know for sure if his helicopter's still there."

She stared at him with wide eyes as he stood from the table.

"I need to make some calls. I'll be back." He paused before leaving the room. "You've done great. Can I get you some more water while you wait?"

She shook her head. "No. Thank you."

He stepped into the empty hallway. There were a lot people who needed waking up. He turned on his computer when he got back to his desk. Before he made any calls, there was something he needed to check.

When he returned to the interview room, the woman's eyes were dry.

"A search effort is underway for Summer. If you're up for it, I'd like you to show me where Colton fired the gun tonight. There might be evidence like gun casings that need to be recovered. The couple that brought you here left their phone number and address, so we'll start there and retrace your steps."

She stood, and he noticed how tall she was for the first time. About the same height as Tess. He held the door open for her. As she moved past, her long blonde curls also reminded him of his wife.

"So, you think this is where you were when he fired the first shot?"

She bit her lip as Stephenson shone his large flashlight beam around the base of the forest. The sun was nearly up, but the thickly wooded area would still be dark for another hour or two.

"I'm sorry. It's so hard to tell. But it looks about right."

"Okay. And the shots came from the direction of the

airport?"

She nodded. Two crime scene investigators trotted past them, each being pulled by a cadaver dog. She looked up at Stephenson with wide eyes.

A look of confusion washed over her face. Confusion that bordered on anger. "What's going on?"

"These dogs are trained to find things like shell casings."

"Oh, okay." Her face seemed to relax.

Stephenson saw Adams approach and he waved his partner over to where they stood.

"Sorry I wasn't here earlier."

Adams had finally answered his phone when Stephenson called him on the ride over. Like Stephenson had figured, his partner had turned his phone off for the night since they weren't on call.

"This is my partner, Detective Kyle Adams."

She weakly returned Adams's handshake. Stephenson was halfway through bringing Adams up to speed when one of the crime scene investigators called out in the distance.

"Stephenson!"

Stephenson turned and held up his hand. "You better stay here with Detective Adams. Just until I see what they've found."

She nodded and took a step back toward his partner.

Stephenson broke into a run when he saw four investigators huddled over a swamp. One took photos with their phone, while another held the search dogs back from the murky water. Stephenson's mind went straight to Tess when he watched two of them pulling a woman's body from the swamp by her bare legs.

His heart sank when he saw the color of her hair. He almost called Tess's name when he came to an abrupt stop over the woman's body. He took in the dead woman's petite frame and was filled with relief, but his respite was quickly replaced by guilt for feeling anything but sadness at the horrific scene.

The young woman had been shot twice at close range, once in the forehead and another in the chest. From her skin color and lack of bloating present, he guessed she'd only been dead a few hours.

"The dogs led us straight to her," one of the investigators said. "There was a large tree branch lying over the swamp that covered her when we found her."

The woman's small frame made her look young, possibly a teenager. She looked to have been shot execution style. Her killer would've been standing right next to her when they shot her in cold blood.

There were a couple of small holes in the girl's tattered leggings that could've happened when she was chased through the woods. Her white sweater was stained with blood and murk from the swamp. Small pieces of green algae covered her entire body.

Stephenson brought up Portia Grenalli's driver's license photo on his phone. According to her license, Portia Grenalli was twenty-two and weighed one hundred and ten pounds. This woman was rail thin, probably under one hundred pounds. It was hard to compare the pretty, smiling woman in the photo with the mottled, ashen-gray corpse with a bullet wound in the middle of her forehead. But they shared the same delicate features. He turned around, making sure the woman pretending to be Portia hadn't followed them.

He texted Adams. *Don't let that woman out of your sight. We just found a body.*

"I'll be right back," Stephenson said to one of the investigators.

When he found Adams, his partner was on his phone. And he was alone.

"Where's the witness?" Stephenson yelled.

Adams looked up at Stephenson marching toward him. He flashed Stephenson a look of annoyance at his interruption and held a finger in the air to signal his partner to wait.

Stephenson pulled Adams's phone away from his ear. "Where is she?"

"Hey! I'm talking to McKinnon."

Stephenson gripped Adams by the shoulders. "Where is she?"

"She had to go to the bathroom." Adams shook his partner's hands away. "I told her there was a female officer right back there who could help her find one."

Stephenson ran in the direction Adams had pointed to and found a female officer standing at the base of the trail.

"Did you just see a tall blonde woman?"

She shook her head. "No. The last person to come through here was Detective Adams."

"Dammit!" Stephenson ran back down the hill toward his partner. Adams was sliding his phone into his jacket pocket when Stephenson found him.

"Did you see which way she went?"

"No. Why are you freaking out?"

"She lied," Stephenson said. "We just found a body in the swamp. A young woman."

Adams started to say something when they heard the rhythmic whir of a helicopter. The detectives exchanged a look as they registered what the sound could mean.

Stephenson tilted his head to see a small black chopper ascending beyond the trees. It climbed in altitude and headed north before it disappeared from their view.

"All helicopters were supposed to be grounded from Boeing Field until we checked to make sure Everett's aircraft wasn't there. I need to call air traffic control."

His phone rang as he pulled it from his pocket. Not recognizing the number, he put the phone to his ear.

"Detective Stephenson."

"This is Commander Appleton with the Coast Guard search and rescue. We just recovered the body of a blonde female matching the description you gave us. We found her near the north shore of Camano Island. Also, one of our helicopters has just now spotted another body off the shore of Whidbey Island. That one also looks female, with long dark hair. We're working to recover the body, so we'll send you a better description soon."

After hanging up, Stephenson filled Adams in on what Portia's imposter had said about Summer Channing and the Coast Guard's findings.

"Call Boeing Field's air traffic control and find out where that helicopter took off from, and if they had permission." Stephenson said before bringing his phone to his ear.

"Okay. Who are you calling?"

"Lieutenant Wallace from the Intel Unit. We need to get to Everett's Whidbey Island property before anyone else gets killed."

Including my wife.

"I'm sure she's fine," Adams said as if reading Stephenson's thoughts.

Stephenson nodded at his partner as the lieutenant's phone rang in his ear.

CHAPTER THIRTY-SIX

Tess awoke with a start to see a dark figure standing beside her bed. She sat up as the figure placed a cold, delicate hand on her arm.

"Colton wants to see you."

It took Tess a moment to remember where she was. She didn't recognize the soft female voice, except she knew it wasn't Avery or Violet. She turned to see her roommate sleeping next to her.

"Follow me," the girl said.

Tess slipped out of bed and thought back to hiding Portia in the back of Colton's helicopter. She'd lain awake for a long time, praying Portia had made it safely to the police department. Tess was surprised that she'd actually fallen asleep.

She followed the girl out of her room and down the quiet hallway until they reached the double doors to Colton's room. The girl opened one of the doors and held it wide for Tess. From the soft light inside Colton's room, Tess recognized the girl as Georgina. Tess paused before going through the doorway.

She wondered what it meant that Colton wanted to see

her in the middle of the night. Had Avery found Portia and returned to punish her? Had she been found out? Or was he using Avery's absence as an opportunity to have Tess *serve* him? She hoped it was the latter. It would be the easiest to find a way out of.

The door closed behind her as soon as Tess stepped through the doorway. The large room was empty. The king-size four poster bed was made and a large fur blanket lay atop the white duvet.

When she snuck in to steal Colton's gun, there hadn't been time to take in the room. The room was much larger than the others she'd seen. It looked almost twice the size of the room she shared with Violet.

Red velvet curtains hung beside each of the three windows. There was a large living area next to the fireplace and a small office space on the other side of the room. Two large computer monitors sat atop an antique mahogany desk.

"Colton?"

"I'm in here." His voice echoed off the marble in the en suite bathroom.

She moved slowly toward the open doorway.

"Hi." Colton smiled from a claw-foot tub when she came into his view. "Come have a seat."

He motioned to a stool next to the bathtub. Water dripped onto the marble floor from his long muscular arm.

There was no sign of Avery. Tess hoped that meant Portia had been able to escape. She wondered what time it was. She guessed somewhere between midnight and three a.m. Which meant, if Portia made it, she should've found Blake by now.

"I'm okay right here," she said.

He let out a short laugh. "Oh, come on. Don't be a prude. We're family now. And I'm not going to yell at you in the doorway."

He wouldn't have to yell. She was only a few feet away. But, she supposed, if she was going to play her part, she'd have to pick her battles carefully. Though she hoped to only be in the castle until her backup arrived in the morning. She uncrossed her arms and moved toward the tub.

He lay back against the white porcelain, smiling as she came toward him. The stool was right next to the tub, on the opposite end to Colton's head. As she sat down, she had a full view of Colton's naked body stretched out in the clear water. Although she tried to maintain eye contact, it was impossible not to take in the rest of him in her periphery.

He bent one of his outstretched legs, opening his groin as he pressed his knee against the edge of the tub. Tess cleared her throat after her eyes followed the movement.

"What did you want to talk to me about?"

"I got an unsettling message from Avery tonight after she left."

Tess was now fully awake. "What did she say?"

Colton adjusted his position again in the tub. Tess pursed her lips.

"She said you weren't to be trusted. And that she would help me deal with you when she gets back in the morning."

His eyes bore into hers.

"Was that all she said?"

"Yes. I asked her why she would say that, but she didn't reply. So, you tell me. Why would she say that?"

"I don't know."

"You know what I think? I think she's jealous of you."

"Jealous?"

"Yes. She sees the way I look at you. I know you feel it too. We have something, you and me. A connection that I've never felt with Avery. I know now that I was wrong to take her back after we went on that date. She threw herself at me when she found out that I'd gone out with you. And I was a fool to allow her back in."

Tess felt sick to her stomach. If Avery had found Portia hiding in the helicopter, what would she have done? Tess also wondered if Avery would have been that cryptic with Colton. Or did he know what Tess had done?

Without warning, Colton stood from the tub and stepped over the edge, exposing himself inches from her face. Her words caught in her throat as water dripped from his body onto her thighs.

"Excuse me," he said as he bent toward her, grabbing a towel from behind her head.

Tess leaned back. She stood from the stool as he stepped back to towel off.

"I have something I want to show you," he said.

"I think I've seen enough." Tess turned and walked out the bathroom, wanting to punch him in the face.

"Tess. Wait." He followed her out of the bathroom and enclosed his grip around her arm. "Don't go yet. I need to show you something."

She stopped, staring at his bedroom door. This felt like a trap. She clenched her jaw and turned around, glad to see he'd had the decency to wrap his towel around his waist. His perfectly muscled chest was still damp.

"Can I trust you?"

His voice was soft. He was so close she could feel the warmth from his body. She looked into his deep blue eyes, and for a moment, she thought he was going to kiss her. She stepped back.

"Yes."

He opened a door next to his desk. She'd assumed it was a closet, but saw it was another small room. There was a bed in the middle with a red bedspread. A small stack of papers sat at the foot of the bed.

He flicked on a dim light. His fingers slid down her arm and grabbed her hand. He stepped into the room and gently pulled her toward him.

"Will you prove it to me? That I can trust you?"

"How?"

He smiled. "Don't worry. I won't force you to sleep with me if you're not ready."

She took a step toward him, and he shut the door behind her. She noticed there was an opened door on the other side of the bed, but she couldn't tell what was beyond it.

"None of the other girls have ever been in here. It's a room only for Avery and me." He sat on the bed and patted the spot beside him. "Our special place." He lifted his hands to make air quotes around the phrase. "But what Avery and I have isn't special. I feel things for you that I've never felt for her. And she's starting to notice. Which is why I think she sent me that text saying not to trust you. Unless there's something you want to tell me."

Tess shook her head. If Colton was doubting Avery's honesty, denial seemed the best course of action. It might at the least buy her time.

"Good." Colton stood from the bed and grabbed the stack of papers off the bedspread. "I want to believe you. I *do* believe you. I think you and I could do great things together. But if I'm going to tell Avery she's a liar, I want to be sure. Are you willing to prove your loyalty to me?"

"How would I do that?" she asked, thinking of the nude photos some of the women had been asked to give up.

He stepped through the doorway on the opposite side of the bed. Tess looked around the room in Colton's absence. The walls were painted a dark gray. A collection of handcuffs hung on the wall beside the bed. They were different styles: one set had tassles, another sparkles, and another was adorned with large feathers. Tess took in the two small decorative knives that looked to be hundreds of years old hung in the shape of an X on the adjacent wall. She heard electronic equipment start up and hum in the next room, and then a bank of studio lights came on.

Curious but on guard, she approached the room where Colton had disappeared. As Tess entered the small space, she saw it was a recording studio. A glass partition divided the room in two. Tess moved through the control room, noticing a door that likely led to the main upstairs hallway. Colton waited for her inside the studio where a tripod was set up facing a stool.

He outstretched his arm. "Read this."

"What is this?" she asked, accepting the pages of printed text.

Her eyes scanned the words when he didn't answer. It was a bunch of profanity-ridden hate speech against the Seattle Police Department. A rant of rage. She flipped the page over and saw that it wasn't just hate speech, but accusations. Criminal accusations of corruption within a few specific investigative units. And accusations against the Seattle mayor and Chief of Police.

"I want you to read it," he said. "on a video recording."

Tess tossed the papers aside. "No."

"I'm not going to show it to anyone. As soon as we're

done, I'll pull the SD card and it will be kept in a locked safe. No one will ever know. It is solely your insurance to me that I can trust you. With anything," Colton said.

Collateral. "So, you'll keep it in case I ever decide to leave the—" she almost said cult but stopped herself. "Organization. Is that right?"

Colton shook his head. "You are free to leave the organization whenever you wish. Something like this would only surface if we were, for some reason, subject to a criminal investigation."

His eyes bore into hers.

"Which would be highly unlikely," he added. "The foundation of EverChange's teaching is trust. I want to make sure I can trust you. That's all. I have no intention of ever showing this to anyone. But for us to make progress, I need this from you. The choice is yours."

Tess's eyes fell to the pages next to her. The accusations written on them were serious. Damaging. And specific. She doubted there was any truth to them, but they might elicit an inquiry if the video was ever made public. But what else could she do? If she refused, Colton would believe Avery.

And if Avery had found Portia, that meant Blake wasn't on his way after all. She prayed she hadn't sent Portia to her death.

"Okay. I'll read it."

"Great."

Colton leaned over and picked up the papers strewn on the floor then pressed a button on top of the camera. He smoothed out the papers and gently handed them back to Tess.

"All right. You're on."

CHAPTER THIRTY-SEVEN

"And in all of this corruption and criminal interference in police proceedings, Governor Green is 100 percent complicit."

Tess let the printed pages fall to her lap. She felt sickened by the words she'd read. The extent of depravity of some of the accusations, even though false, made her stomach turn that she'd said them aloud. And on camera.

The door flung open behind Colton. Avery's eyes narrowed as she looked at Colton and then at Tess. Tess had been so sickened by the words she'd read inside the recording studio that she hadn't heard Avery's helicopter land.

Colton's demeanor did a one-eighty at the sight of his fiancé. He looked like a scared child about to be scolded.

"Avery. I thought you weren't coming back until the morning."

She eyed Tess with disgust. "I can see that. And, technically, it is morning."

Unlike when Tess saw her last night, Avery's hair was a tangled mess. Mascara was smeared under her eyes. She looked like she'd been through much more than a helicopter ride. It was all Tess could do not to ask about Portia.

Colton swallowed hard. "Tess was just proving her loyalty to Everchange by reading some dirt on the Seattle PD."

Avery gave him a cold smile. "I know." She pointed to the corner of the ceiling behind Tess.

Tess cocked her head to see a small camera mounted in the corner of the room.

"You forgot to turn it off," Avery said. She stepped into the room and closed the door behind her. "I heard it all."

Tess had never seen Colton look anything but confident. Now his face was ruled by fear. He reached for Avery, but she slapped his hands away.

"Please. Avery. This is a misunderstanding. After you texted me I—I wanted to give Tess a chance to explain herself."

" I've hand-fed you almost every girl here. There's only one I asked you to keep your distance from. *One.* If I can't trust you, I have no use for you anymore."

Avery's bloodshot eyes were wide with rage. She stormed out of the studio with Colton on her heels. Avery swiped a knife off the wall as Tess followed them out the studio door. In one swift motion, she pivoted and extended her arm. Tess watched the dagger slice through Colton's neck.

Blood gushed from his deep open wound as he fell to the ground. Tess dropped to her knees beside him. His throat gurgled as his warm blood soaked the floor under Tess's bare legs.

"Colton!"

Tess yanked the bedspread off the edge of the bed and used it to put pressure on his gaping wound. But there was no stopping it. The thick fabric was saturated seconds after she pressed it against his neck. The life was already gone from his eyes.

"It's no use." Avery stood over her, knife still in hand. "You can't save him. He's gone."

Tess's eyes moved to the other dagger still hanging on the wall.

Avery pressed her bloody knife into the base of Tess's jaw. "Don't even think about it."

Avery stepped back and snatched the other blade that Tess had been eyeing. With a knife in each hand, Avery bent beside Tess. She held the tip of one blade less than an inch from Tess's chin.

Tess looked down at her hands, covered with Colton's blood. All the color was gone from his face. *Like Chris.*

An image of her brother filled Tess's mind. Pale with a gaping, bloody neck wound and a massive pool of blood under his body.

Tess's chest wall tightened as she tried to fight off the crippling anxiety that threatened to overtake her. It was becoming harder to draw air into her lungs.

"Where is Portia?" Tess managed to say. Although she feared she already knew the answer.

Avery let out a lighthearted laugh. "Last I saw her she was in a swamp near Boeing Field with a couple bullets in her. But I think your boyfriend may've found her. So, she might be on her way to a medical examiner's office by now."

Tess could hardly breathe. She made the mistake of looking at Colton's lifeless eyes before turning away.

Avery stood to her feet, tucking one of the daggers under her arm. She swiped a set of feathered handcuffs off the wall before she leaned over and pressed the knife into

Tess's clavicle. She snapped one of the cuffs around Tess's wrist before she yanked her arm and clamped the other cuff onto the bed rail. Her face was close enough that Tess could feel her breath when she spoke.

"I'm going to let the women know that you've killed their beloved leader. And when they hear how you murdered him, a man they would give their lives for, they're going to eat you alive."

Avery tossed the bloody dagger onto the bed, keeping a tight grip on the other in her left hand. She backed out the door and closed it behind her. Instead of trying to break free, Tess was frozen in place, hovering over Colton's dead body. *Why can't I breathe?*

But she knew why. She felt the familiar symptoms of a panic attack taking over her body. Though it had been nearly a year, she still felt the pain of her younger brother's death as if it was yesterday.

She bent over and placed her hand on her thigh. She was light-headed. Her temples throbbed as she sucked in short, shallow gasps of air. The original herringbone floor was spinning underneath her as she dropped to her knees. She needed her pills.

Her chest ached in a way that made her wonder if she might be having a heart attack. She clutched her chest as tears streamed down her face.

She heard Avery scream at the women from the nearby hallway. "Wake up! Colton's dead!"

Tess tried unsuccessfully to pull free from the feathered handcuffs. She leaned back and kicked the cuff attached to the bedframe. Pain resounded through her heel as she heard something snap. She bent her knee and slammed her heel into the cuff a second time and the flimsy cuff broke open.

With the other cuff still around her wrist, Tess forced herself to stand. She put her hand on the end of the bed to steady herself. She opened the door with her bloody hands to the main part of Colton's room. The landline had been severed on top of Colton's desk.

Avery's voice resounded down the hall. She sounded hysterical. Tess could hear voices from the women who'd been jolted awake by Avery's call to arms. They'd be trying to break Colton's door down any second. Tess ran to the double doors and turned the lock.

She rushed to the antique dresser and swung open three drawers in search of Avery's Lamborghini key fob. The only keys Tess found were on a retro keychain with a Ferrari symbol. They would have to do.

She grabbed the keys and a Fendi sunglasses case before she ran to the wardrobe and pulled out one of Avery's oversized sweaters. Tess pulled it on as she ran into the bathroom, closing and locking the door behind her.

She heard banging on the bedroom doors as she pressed her hands against the base of window above the toilet. The window opened only an inch before getting stuck. She stood on the toilet seat and pulled with all her might, but it wouldn't budge. She could hear screaming from inside Colton's room. Tess took a deep breath and used the force of her body weight to shove the window open. The rail smacked against the top of the window frame with a loud crack.

The screams had almost reached the bathroom when Tess climbed out, one leg at a time, and swung herself out the second-story window. There was no ledge. The exterior castle wall went straight down to the hedges below.

She hung from the windowsill by her fingertips for only

a second before letting go. She landed hard in the small hedges that lined the house, but her adrenaline kept her from feeling the cuts from the branches on her bare legs.

She got to her feet and ran around the side of the house through the early-morning fog.

"I see her! She went out the window!" Tess heard a woman call from above before she rounded the corner of the castle.

When she reached the detached garage, Tess tried the side door. She'd been prepared to kick it open, but it opened with ease.

She figured this shouldn't have surprised her as she ran through the garage. With a gated and guarded entrance, the girls couldn't simply steal a car and drive out of the compound. *Unless they could pass for Avery driving Colton's car.*

CHAPTER THIRTY-EIGHT

Avery ran into the bathroom when she heard Violet call out. Violet stood on the toilet with her head hanging out the open window. She turned and stepped down when she heard Avery behind her.

"There was just enough light for me to see her run around the corner of the house," Violet said.

Avery heard the unmistakable sounds of a helicopter. She leapt onto the toilet seat and peered out over the bluffs. The lights from two helicopters flying in formation were making their way across the bay. Straight for the castle.

She jumped down and grabbed Violet by the shoulders. Sobs from two other women filled the bathroom before Avery could speak.

"Why would she do this to him?" Tears streamed down Georgina's face. Her blood-soaked hands were shaking.

The girl who stood next to her was crying too hard to talk. She wrapped her arms around the supermodel and let out a loud wail.

Avery returned her focus to Violet. She was glad to see the reality star's eyes were filled with hatred. And determination.

"I'll go after Tess," Avery said, aware of the police helicopter's rotor blades growing louder. "Tess killed Colton and she's trying to pin his death on us." She made sure her voice was loud enough for the other women to hear. "The police are coming. Don't let them come in. Defend our castle."

"That bitch!" one of the girls called from beyond the bathroom doors.

Avery held back a smile. It was good to hear anger stirring amongst the women and not just sadness. She needed them to rise up and fight.

"Okay." Violet nodded. "We will."

Avery let go of the redhead's shoulders. "Get your shotgun. Save our home. Our reputation." She raised her voice as she pushed through the grieving pair blocking the bathroom doorway. "They'll try to take our home. Don't let them. The castle is ours to protect. It's what Colton would've wanted. It's too late to save his life, but we can save everything he stood for. Grab your weapons! If you don't have a gun, grab a sword or axe from the walls."

Avery couldn't stop her smile as she raced down the hallway. She could sense the power she'd created as the girls rushed to arm themselves. To transform into an army that would rise in her defense.

There would be no more hiding behind Colton's façade. *She* was their leader now.

CHAPTER THIRTY-NINE

Tess rushed past a yellow Lamborghini and used the larger key on the keychain to unlock the driver's door to Colton's classic red Ferrari. She felt a new rush of anxiety as she climbed in next to the tall silver gearshift. She hadn't driven a stick since she was seventeen. And even then she wasn't great at driving a manual. She took a deep breath to calm herself as she slid on Avery's oversized sunglasses and pressed the garage door opener clipped to the visor above her head.

Tess slid the key into the dash and, with one foot on the clutch and the other on the brake, she turned the ignition. The sports car's engine rumbled to life. She grabbed the ball of the gearshift with her left hand and mistakenly put it into reverse, thinking it was first. The car lurched backward in the garage. Tess slammed on the brakes, recalling what Avery had told her about the gearshift pattern when they went for a drive.

She slid the gearshift to the lower left corner, let up on the clutch, and moved her foot to the gas pedal. The car lurched forward before the engine died.

She swore as she stepped on the clutch and restarted the

car. She glanced at the side door to the garage. It was still closed.

She slid the gearshift down to the left and tried again. This time, the car eased forward as she took her foot off the clutch. She gave it more gas after pulling out of the garage. All Avery would need to do was look out the window to see Tess trying to escape in Colton's car.

Okay. You've got this.

She kept it in first as she drove toward the guard at the end of the drive. Tess recognized the short brunette as Camilla. The gate was closed. Camilla would've heard the helicopter return with Avery. Tess hoped she might open the gate when she recognized Colton's car with what Tess prayed looked like Avery behind the wheel. But the gate didn't open when she approached.

She slid the gearshift to neutral, trying not to kill the engine as she stopped the car next to the celebrity chef. She couldn't afford to look like she couldn't drive a manual. Camilla peered at her through the window of the Ferrari.

Why isn't she opening the gate? Tess forced a smile. Camilla reached into her back pocket, pulled out a small tablet, and tapped a button. The front gate began to open. Tess tried to keep her hand from shaking as she placed it back on the gearshift.

Camilla gave her a curt nod. Tess waited for the gate to fully open before she moved the car into first. *Don't kill the engine, don't kill the engine.*

Camilla's radio made a loud crackle. She pulled it from her pocket and held it in front of her mouth. "Can you repeat that?"

"Camilla!" Tess recognized Avery's voice come over Camilla's radio. "This is Avery. Don't—"

Tess stepped on the gas. The Ferrari's engine revved over the sound of Camilla's radio. She let out the clutch, and the car's tires squealed before it jumped forward. She fish-tailed through the gate as the tires struggled to gain traction. There was no other car in sight when she pulled onto the two-lane road and successfully shifted into second.

She'd made it out. Barely. Now, she needed to call the lieutenant and get her to organize a tactical unit ASAP. She just needed to get to a phone.

She checked the rearview mirror as she shifted to third and saw Camilla running after her. The chef stopped in the middle of the road and aimed her rifle at the Ferrari. Tess heard the blast from the gun just before a bullet shattered the passenger side mirror.

Tess sank lower into her seat and sped toward a bend up ahead. The sound of tires screeching tore Tess's attention away from the road. She checked her rearview mirror again as she threw the Ferrari into fourth.

Camilla had lowered her gun. And Avery's Lamborghini had just peeled out of the compound.

CHAPTER FORTY

Tess shifted to maneuver through the tight bend in the road while Avery's Lamborghini closed in on her from behind. Tess drifted into the oncoming lane as she took the corner too fast.

Tess moved back into the right lane as the road straightened out. She shifted into third while Avery slowed to make the corner behind her.

She sped toward a stop sign up ahead where the road came to a T. She glanced in her rearview mirror, seeing Avery gaining on her once again. Tess downshifted when she neared the stop sign. She slowed just long enough to look in both directions before she pulled onto the two-lane highway in front of an oncoming semi-truck.

The old Ferrari's engine revved when Tess floored the accelerator, while Avery was stuck waiting for the semi to pass. Moss-covered tree branches hung low over the road. She shifted back into third as Avery's Lamborghini turned onto the highway.

The Lamborghini was gaining on her as Tess sped over a narrow bridge above a creek. Tess knew she was coming up on the Deception Pass Bridge, but there was too much fog up ahead for her to see it.

There was a blur of movement in her peripheral vision. Tess turned to see Avery's Lamborghini had pulled up next to her in the oncoming lane. Tess and Avery's eyes met for a split second. Tess started to shift into fourth when Avery's car slammed into the side of the Ferrari, forcing it into the guardrail. Tess gripped the steering wheel with both hands as metal screeched against metal.

Tess jerked the car back into her lane as she collided with the Lamborghini. She steered to the right and downshifted to regain her speed as the tree-lined highway gave way to the Deception Pass Bridge. She pressed the gas pedal to the floor as the Ferrari sped ahead of the Lamborghini.

A white haze encompassed the bridge on either side, blocking the view of the water nearly two hundred feet below. A horn blared before the headlights from a pickup became visible through the fog in the oncoming lane. Tess watched Avery's headlights pull into the lane behind her seconds before the pickup sped past them.

The fog cleared enough for Tess to see she'd nearly reached the island that separated the two spans of the Deception Pass Bridge. The Lamborghini's engine roared as Avery swerved another time into the oncoming lane. Tess braced herself for impact when Avery pulled beside her. But, instead of ramming her into the guardrail, Avery sped forward, overtaking the Ferrari with an incredible speed which Tess's Ferrari couldn't match.

Avery disappeared into a sheet of white fog. Tess's visibility was next to nothing as she let up on the gas and pushed the gearshift up to fourth. *Was Avery making an escape?* Was she going to let Tess go that easily? After all she'd done, Tess couldn't let her get away.

Tess was surrounded by a bleak, blinding white, but she kept her foot on the gas. In an instant, the fog cleared to reveal two sets of headlights speeding in her direction. One set was in the oncoming lane. The other, belonging to Avery's Lamborghini, raced toward Tess beside the delivery truck.

The truck laid on its horn. Tess had only seconds to react before impact. She yanked the steering wheel to the left, crossing the oncoming lane. She felt the gust of wind from the two vehicles speeding by as the Ferrari plummeted over the edge of the steep rocky island before the start of the second bridge.

Her hands searched for something to hold onto as the car rolled down the cliff. She felt momentarily weightless before she was jerked backward by her shoulder strap. Her head smacked against the door. Her world spun as the car continued to roll.

The passenger window shattered on impact with the rocky hill. Her jaw slammed against the steering wheel. She raised her arms to protect her head against the terrain that came through her open driver's window on the final roll before the car flew off the edge of the island into the strait.

The car landed upside down and Tess hung from her seatbelt as frigid water flooded the car, her head pressed against the roof. Tess drew in a deep breath before the salt water immersed her head completely.

She held her breath as the floor of the car sank closer to the water level. She felt frantically for her seatbelt buckle. Her hands ran across her torso until she felt the cold metal clip. Her seatbelt was already underwater as she pressed against the buckle with her thumb. She blew a small amount of air out her nose to keep it from filling with water as she struggled to free herself from the safety harness.

The car sank faster as more water poured in. Her lungs longed to let out the breath she fought to hold in. Using both hands, she pressed and pulled on the buckle. When it didn't budge, she tugged harder. But her strength was fading fast. She forced herself to focus against the paralyzing panic that threatened to overtake her.

She thought of Blake and knew she had too much to live for than to die inside this car. She clawed at the buckle and tugged on the strap with as much force as she could muster, knowing her time for escaping this death trap was running out.

The belt came free as the floor of the car sank beneath the water's surface. More air escaped her nose as Tess pushed the strap aside. She stretched her arms through the opened window as the hood of the car sank toward the ocean floor. She blew out the breath she'd been holding as she swam to the surface.

Tess gasped for air when her head rose from the water. Strong currents ripped through the narrow waterway between the island and the mainland. Her body was pulled under the bridge as she struggled to swim to the shore. She knew she wouldn't survive long in the Sound's cold waters and fought through the developing hypothermia that slowed her movements.

She'd made it only a few strokes closer to the rocky shore when she came out under the other side of the bridge. Her movements slowed from the cold, and the current dragged her faster.

"Ahh!" she groaned when the current slammed her against a group of large rocks protruding from the water beside the island. She raised her freezing hands out of the water and pulled herself onto the rocks.

"Stay there! Help is on the way!"

She clung to the rocks as she looked up to the bridge in the direction of the man's voice. She could barely make out a figure though the fog, but she didn't have the strength to respond.

"Hang on! I'm calling for help!"

Tess shivered as she lay against the rocks, taking in short, shallow breaths. She was filled with resolve as an image of Avery slicing open Colton's throat flashed in her mind. Avery had to be stopped. And she'd do everything in her power to ensure that evil woman never hurt anyone again.

CHAPTER FORTY-ONE

Stephenson looked out the window of the police helicopter as it descended upon the Whidbey Island property. Detective Ben Suarez, Tess's old homicide partner, sat to his left and two SWAT detectives sat across from them. A thin layer of fog hovered above the immaculate grounds, giving the Gothic structure an eerie glow in the early morning light. The chopper landed smoothly on the lawn and, without a word, the four detectives withdrew their firearms from their holsters.

A second police helicopter landed beside them carrying more SWAT detectives and Lieutenant Wallace from Intel, who had insisted on coming. Stephenson and Suarez followed the SWAT detectives out the chopper and jumped onto the grass with their guns ready. Stephenson was glad to see Wallace remain in the helicopter as the four SWAT detectives appeared on the lawn beside them. It had likely been a couple of decades since she'd been in a tactical situation that wasn't behind a desk.

As they approached the castle, a shot rang out from an upper story window and struck a SWAT detective in her bulletproof vest. She staggered backward from the bullet's impact. Two SWAT detectives in the front lifted their ballistic shields in the direction of the window as the others tucked in behind them. There was nowhere else for the detectives to take cover. Another shot rang out from the castle, sending chunks of sod into the air next to Stephenson as they returned fire.

When Stephenson reached the patio, he could make out a dark-haired woman leaning out an upstairs window with a long rifle pointing straight at him. He fixed his sights on her and fired. Another woman with a smaller gun was perched in a window next to her. A shot rang out from the castle and exploded into the stamped concrete in front of the detectives.

Stephenson and the detectives fired more shots before he watched the two wounded women fall away from the second-story windows. The dark-haired woman's rifle fell from her grip and clamored against the patio below.

"You okay?" Suarez asked the SWAT detective who'd taken a bullet to her vest.

She nodded. "I'm good."

They ascended the patio steps as a woman with flaming red hair came around the side of the castle with a shotgun under her arm. She pointed the barrel at Stephenson and pumped the slide. Stephenson fired two rounds into her shoulder and chest, sending her backward as she fired a slug into the sky.

Her firearm fell away from her hand when she hit the ground. Stephenson ran to her side and used his foot to slide it out of her reach. She groaned as she lay semiconscious in her silk nightgown, identical to what Andrea Morris had been wearing.

Another woman came around the corner, holding an

antique dagger in her hand. Suarez and Stephenson fixed their weapons on her as she dropped to the ground next to the redhead.

"Violet!"

"Drop your weapon!" Stephenson yelled.

The girl sobbed while she knelt over her friend, still holding tight to the large knife.

Stephenson took a step toward her with his gun aimed at her chest. "I said drop your weapon!" He inched closer. "Drop it *now*!"

The girl threw the blade onto the ground and stroked her friend's hair. A SWAT detective moved around and swiftly cuffed her hands behind her back while she cried hysterically over the other woman.

"I got this. You guys go," the SWAT detective said.

Stephenson nodded and turned for the patio doors while Suarez and three SWAT detectives moved around the side of the castle to secure the outside perimeter. After trying the doorknob of the French patio doors, Stephenson stepped aside to make room for a SWAT member to swing her battering ram into the door.

The door flew open with a crack and Stephenson followed the two SWAT detectives inside.

They were met with a scream as a woman came flying over a couch with a battle-axe above her head. She wore the same tiny silk nightgown as the others and launched herself toward the SWAT detective in front of Stephenson.

The shot from the SWAT detective's 9mm echoed in Stephenson's ears as the woman dropped to the floor.

"Ahhh!" the woman screamed from the bullet in her shoulder as she rolled on the hardwood floor.

The detective knelt next to her, sliding the double-headed axe out of her reach. Two more women, clad in matching silk nightgowns, appeared in the doorway to the living room. One held a rifle with trembling hands, the other held a sword at her side.

"Drop your weapons and place your hands on your head!" Stephenson ordered as he and the other SWAT detective marched toward them.

The girls looked in shock at their friend lying on the floor, crying in pain.

"*Now!*" Stephenson said.

He heard Suarez and SWAT break through the castle's front door before they announced themselves and then their heavy footsteps sounded on the wooden staircase.

The girl lowered her gun with shaking hands as she brought her eyes to the barrel of Stephenson's gun. The rifle and sword clanged against the floor as Stephenson ordered the women to get on their knees with their hands above their heads.

"I'm going to help secure the upstairs." The SWAT detective moved past Stephenson while he finished handcuffing the women.

After securing their cuffs, Stephenson took out his phone and showed them a photo of Tess.

"Have you seen this woman?"

They stared at the photo in silence.

"I know you have. Where is she?"

"I don't know," one of them finally said.

"Don't say any more," the other girl told her. "We're not talking without an attorney."

"Fine."

Stephenson left them with the other SWAT detective and headed for the stairs. When he got to the staircase, two

SWAT detectives were leading three women in short silk nightgowns down the steps.

None of them were Tess.

"Are there more people upstairs?" he asked.

"Just the two women who were shooting at us. One still has a pulse. Our guys got an armed woman to surrender her weapon at the front gate, so I'll give them the okay to send the medic units through while we check the rest of the property," the female SWAT detective said. She had her hand around a girl's arm as she led her to the bottom of the steps. "There's also a deceased male in one of the bedrooms. Throat's been slit. Detective Suarez is up there with one of our SWAT detectives. Looks like it might be Colton Everett."

"Any sign of Detective Richards?"

The SWAT detective shook her head. The tactical team had all been shown a photo of Tess before they arrived. It was part of their mission to find her and get her out safely.

"Did you ask them?" He motioned toward the three women in handcuffs.

"We did. We showed them her photo. But they're refusing to talk."

Stephenson bolted up the stairs, taking them two at time. *Where was Tess?*

"Suarez?" Stephenson called when he reached the top of the staircase.

"I'm down here," he heard Suarez call.

With his gun at his side, Stephenson moved cautiously down the long hallway lined with ornate doors and Renaissance art. Suarez appeared at the end of the hall.

"This way." With a latex-gloved hand, he motioned for Stephenson to follow him through the double doors.

Stephenson followed him inside the large bedroom and into a small adjoining room where Colton Everett lay covered in blood. Stephenson stopped inside the doorway, careful not to step in the puddle that surrounded Everett's body. There was a bloody dagger with a decorative silver handle on the middle of the bed.

"I already took some photos," Suarez said. "CSI is on their way."

"She's in the bathroom," Stephenson turned to see a SWAT detective leading medics through the bedroom.

"You think Tess did this?" Suarez stared down at the bloody corpse. "In self-defense?"

"My guess would be Avery. She would've had time after she came back in the helicopter. And she already tried to pin two murders on him." Stephenson's eyes scanned the room and stopped when he saw a small camera mounted in the corner. He pointed to the camera. "If we're lucky, there might be footage of the murder."

A voice crackled through their radios. "We found two more women in a pole building on the other side of the property."

Stephenson held his breath.

"One of them's in pretty bad shape. She's barely conscious. Looks like she's been locked up for a while and starved. We need a medic unit down here now."

"Any sign of Detective Richards?"

"Negative. But we noticed the detached garage doors were open and two car spots were empty."

"We'll have to take all these women in our two ambulances." Stephenson heard a medic say in the other room. "Two other units were just dispatched to Deception Pass Bridge. There's been a bad accident. Apparently, two cars went over the side into the water."

Stephenson moved to the bathroom doorway where the medics were working on one of the women. She was conscious and looked to have been shot in the neck.

"We passed a Lamborghini and an old sports car on the way here," another medic told the SWAT detectives as they lifted the woman onto the stretcher. "They were flying. Could've been them."

Avery had a Lamborghini registered in her name. And the old sports car could be Colton's classic Ferrari. Stephenson stepped aside to give the medics room as they rolled the woman out of the bathroom on a stretcher.

"Let's get her and the other suspects loaded into the ambulances," the medic said to the other. She turned to the SWAT detective. "Maybe your guys can help us load up the women from the pole building so we can get everyone to hospital as quick as possible."

"For sure," the detective said before getting on his radio.

"What's the status of that accident on Deception Pass?" Stephenson asked as the medics rolled past him.

The emergency responder turned to him. "Sounds like there was one survivor. They're taking her to Island Hospital in Anacortes. She's pretty lucky to have lived through that."

Suarez and Stephenson exchanged a look as the medics rushed the stretcher down the hall.

"It could be Tess," Suarez said.

Or Avery, Stephenson thought. In which case, he needed to get to her before she escaped. Again. But he prayed the survivor was his wife.

He turned to find Lieutenant Wallace standing behind him. He wondered how long she'd been there.

"Tess and Avery aren't here. The medics saw two sports cars speeding toward Deception Pass on their way here. There was an accident on the bridge. A survivor is being taken to Island Hospital. A woman. I need to—"

The lieutenant held up her hand. "I heard. Take one of our helicopters. I'll radio the pilot and let him know you're coming down."

He wasn't expecting her to be so agreeable. "Thank you."

"This is Lieutenant Wallace," he heard her say as he left the room. "We believe either a suspect or an undercover detective has been taken to Island Hospital. Detective Stephenson is headed your way. I want you to get him there, asap."

CHAPTER FORTY-TWO

Stephenson walked through the sliding glass door and pushed aside the gray curtain that hung from the ceiling of Tess's room in the ER. He rushed toward the hospital bed. Tess was conscious and was covered with what looked like a small air mattress.

"Blake." Her voice was weak.

He knelt at her side. "Are you okay?"

"I'm fine. They X-rayed my neck when I got here. It's not broken, just sprained. But I do have a couple of fractured ribs. And some mild hypothermia and a concussion. The doc was amazed my injuries weren't worse. How did you—"

He brought his face to hers and kissed her softly. "I don't know what I would do if you…" his voice trailed off.

"How did you know I was here?"

"I just came from a raid of the EverChange mansion. I heard about two cars going over the Deception Pass Bridge from one of the medics. They said there was a survivor. Since you weren't at the castle, I could only hope it was you."

Tess sat up in the bed. "Wait. Two cars?"

"Yeah. When I got here, the head nurse told me that the guy who called 9-1-1 for you witnessed a yellow Lamborghini also go into the water. It veered off the road and went down the other side of that small island."

"That's what Avery was driving. She chased me after I left the castle. It's why I went off the road. Did she make it out?"

He shook his head. "No. The witness saw the car sink right after you went over the side."

"What if she got out before it went into the water?"

"I don't think there was time. Plus, they've searched the area. She's not there."

"Are they sending divers down to find the car?"

He nodded. "The officer I spoke with on the way here said they are. But it might not be right away. The currents are moving pretty fast through that strait."

She pulled her arm out from under her warming blanket. He placed his hand on hers.

"Don't worry. It's over. Colton and Avery are dead. And we have everyone from the castle in custody."

"How did you know to come to the castle? Did Portia find you?" She prayed Avery had lied about killing her.

"We haven't formally identified her yet, but we found a body near Boeing Field that looks like it's Portia. Avery came to Headquarters and asked to speak with me. She told me she was Portia—"

"Wait. She *what?*" Tess sat up farther and pulled her other arm out from under her blanket.

"She said that Colton had tried to kill her after he landed at Boeing Field. When I took her back to the area where she said he'd fired a gun at her, we found what we believe is Portia's body."

Her eyes brimmed with tears. "Avery told me she killed her. But I hoped she was lying. It's my fault. I—" her voice broke. "I put her on that helicopter."

"It's not your fault."

Tess wiped a tear that fell down her cheek. "Did they find Charity? She was imprisoned in a pole building behind the airplane hangar."

"The SWAT team found two women locked in a pole building. They were being taken to the hospital when I left."

Tess leaned back on her pillow. "Charity wasn't going to make it much longer. She'd been malnourished for a long time. The other woman is Monica Kerry, the famous tennis player. She was guarding that building with a gun and I had to lock her inside while I sent Portia to find you."

"The Coast Guard also recovered a woman's body off the north shore of Camano Island. It—"

"That's Aspen Okamoto. The Olympic skier. She fell from the bluffs the night before last. Colton and Avery tried to cover it up, and they refused to call the authorities."

Stephenson looked confused. "Aspen Okamoto? Isn't she Asian? Dark hair?"

"Yeah."

He shook his head. "This woman was Caucasian. Blonde. From what Avery told me when she came to Headquarters, we believe it's the body of Summer Channing."

Tess winced from the pain when she sat forward. "Summer? Why—what happened?"

"When Avery was impersonating Portia, she said Colton had pushed Summer out the door of the helicopter when they were over the water between the island and the mainland. The Coast Guard found her earlier this morning."

Tess sobbed. "No!"

He hadn't expected her to take it so hard. "I'm sorry, Tess."

He moved to the edge of her bed and carefully enfolded her into his arms. She leaned into him and cried with her head against his chest, reminding him of the night her brother died.

A middle-aged nurse wearing pink scrubs swatted the curtain open and came into the small room.

"Sorry to interrupt," she said flatly as she came toward the bed, "but I need to take your temperature again."

Stephenson kissed the top of her head. "Colton and Avery are dead. They can't hurt anyone anymore. It's over."

The nurse came to a stop next to the bed and Stephenson moved back to a chair at the bedside. Tess let out a loud sniff as she lay back against the bed.

She held his gaze with her tear-filled eyes. "I'll believe that when I see footage of her dead body inside that submerged car."

The nurse impatiently pursed her lips. "Is he your husband?"

A weak smiled escaped Tess's mouth. "Yes."

"It's up to you if you're okay with him staying." She held up the tip of the thermometer's probe. "It's gotta be rectal."

CHAPTER FORTY-THREE

Three days later, Tess flicked on her TV and flipped through the channels. She'd been staring out her bedroom window for the last half hour, for lack of anything else to do. Chloe had insisted on staying during the day until Blake got home from work and she'd been hovering like a hawk making sure Tess didn't overdo it. She wouldn't even allow Tess to make her own food.

As much as she loved her sister-in-law, she couldn't wait for Blake to get home. She couldn't stand being treated like an invalid for much longer. And she needed to get back to work. There was still a lot of work to be done to prove Avery was behind all the killings and abuse inside EverChange. There was also Colton's late wife.

She heard Chloe turn on her vacuum in the living room. Her brother's wife had been shocked to hear about the criminal activities inside EverChange, as well as Colton's death and Tess's role in uncovering the awful truth. Taking care of Tess seemed to be what she needed to take her mind off things, and Tess knew EverChange wasn't the only thing Chloe was trying not think about.

Chris's murder trial ended yesterday afternoon, and the

jury was still deliberating his killer's verdict. Tess scrolled through the TV Guide, hoping for a distraction. Finally, she clicked on the local news.

A familiar local news reporter filled the screen.

"More details are emerging from the multi-million-dollar EverChange compound on Whidbey Island. What seemed to be an exclusive private retreat for some of EverChange's most famous members has turned out to be what some are calling a house of horrors built on blackmail, coercion, forced sex, and even murder. Including the deaths of ex-Olympic skier Aspen Okamoto, Instagram influencer Portia Grenalli, and Oscar-winning actress Summer Channing.

"We'll have more on this special update after our commercial break."

CSI had recovered the SIG Sauer Tess had given to Portia in the swamp where they found Portia's body. It was hard for Tess not to feel guilty when she learned Portia was shot with the very weapon Tess had given her to defend herself. The 9mm had been purchased by Avery, not Colton, which explained why Tess hadn't recalled him being left-handed.

Tess's phone rang atop her bedside table as the news went to commercial. She muted the TV, glad to see it was Blake. Hopefully it meant that divers had found Avery's Lamborghini.

"Hey, babe."

"Hey," he said. "We're going through the data TESU extracted from Avery's phone that was found at the castle. And we've found something big."

The Technical Electronic Support Unit was on the same floor as Homicide and was where they sent all electronic devices to have their data extracted and compiled.

"What?"

"It shows Colton pushing his late wife, Parker, over a cliff on Mount Rainier. He seemed to hesitate when the video started rolling, and Avery can be heard behind the camera asking him what he's waiting for. Then he shoves Parker over the edge.

"She sent the video to Colton's phone several times in the last few years. Looks like she was using it as blackmail."

"Within EverChange, they call that collateral." Hearing this confirmed to Tess that Avery didn't just overtake Colton in the end, but she'd been the mastermind behind EverChange all along. "What about Colton's phone? Did he have any sort of blackmail against Avery?"

"Not that we could find."

"Have the divers found the Lamborghini yet?"

"Umm, no. They've been searching for two days, but the visibility hasn't been great. They still haven't found it, and the currents will be too strong over the next few days for them to go down again. So, they've suspended the search."

"For how long?"

"Indefinitely. There's no hope of saving her life at this point, and they can't justify the risk to the divers."

"What if she got out before the car went into the water?"

Blake breathed into the phone. "There were two witnesses who saw the Lamborghini's bumper become submerged before it sank. There wasn't time for her to get out. And if she had, emergency responders would've found her. Tess...she's gone."

Chloe burst into her room before Tess could respond.

"The jury's back!" she shouted. "We have to go. They have a verdict."

CHAPTER FORTY-FOUR

Three Months Later

"How's Tess liking the Intel Unit?"

Stephenson turned around in his desk chair to face his partner. "She's doing a lot better now that all those EverChange trials are over."

"I bet. Although she seemed a little conflicted about that redhead reality star getting thirty years for your attempted murder and reckless endangerment of that Olympic skier."

"I think she's at peace with it. And knowing her brother's killer got put away for life. She's even mentioned wanting to return to homicide one day. Although, she still has a hard time that we never recovered Avery's body. I think she just wanted more resolution."

Adams pulled out a stick of gum from his pocket. "There's no way Avery survived."

"I know. But I can't seem to explain away that seed of doubt in Tess's mind. She says it's a gut feeling. But I'm sure she'll come to terms with it eventually."

"Well, a gut feeling isn't really something you should ignore," Adams said.

"I agree. Except when it contradicts factual evidence."

Adams phone rang. Stephenson paused for him to

answer. He turned back to his computer screen as Adams lifted the receiver.

"Detective Adams."

Stephenson clicked through his emails, checking the confirmation from the resort in Tahiti where he was taking Tess next week. Now that the EverChange trials were over, he was going to surprise her with a real honeymoon. He'd secretly arranged for Tess's time off with Lieutenant Wallace.

Adams set his phone back onto the receiver and stood from his chair. "Andrea Morris's sister is downstairs and wants to talk to us. She thinks Avery might still be alive."

Savannah's hair was shorter than the last time Stephenson had seen her. And the resolution on Savannah's face at their last meeting was now replaced with worry lines. He and Adams had gone to her apartment to give her the news that they'd found traces of Andrea's DNA under the bumper of one of the SUV's kept at the EverChange Whidbey Island compound. The same SUV he'd found on a downtown traffic camera the night of Andrea's murder. Avery's prints were all over the driver's side. The woman guarding the gate also confirmed that Avery had left the compound in that SUV shortly after Rachelle and didn't return until three hours later.

"I know you've never found Avery's body," she said before the detectives had a chance to sit down. "And I think someone from EverChange is staying at my parents' lake house."

Adams and Stephenson exchanged a quick glance as they took seats in the cheaply padded chairs across from her.

"My parents left us their vacation home on Lake Coeur d'Alene. They had it for years, but I hardly ever go up there. Anyway, the neighbors called me yesterday and said someone's been there. A woman they didn't recognize. They've known Andrea and I since we were kids. They thought it was strange after no one had been there in so long.

"They knocked on the front door, but the woman didn't answer. So, they called me to see if I had a friend staying there, which I don't. I talked to our security system company this morning and they said someone had disarmed the alarm using the keypad over a month ago." Her eyes shot eagerly between the detectives. "Maybe someone at EverChange got our security code from Andrea. Or what if it's Avery?"

"Have you called the Coeur d'Alene Police about this yet?"

Savannah shook her head. "I wanted to speak with you first."

Stephenson stood from his chair. "Thank you. We'll check into it and call the local authorities if we need to. And we'll be in touch with what we find. We might need to pay your houseguest a visit."

The two detectives stepped off the elevator after escorting Savannah out of Police Headquarters.

"Are you gonna tell Tess about this?" Adams asked as they crossed the hall to the Homicide Unit.

"Not until we find out who it is. I don't want to give her a false hope that it could be Avery, you know?"

Suarez was waiting for them at their cubicle.

"You guys need to see something."

They followed Suarez to his desk where he typed

something into his computer.

"Two recreational divers came upon a sunken yellow Lamborghini this afternoon while they were diving Deception Pass. Apparently, one of them already uploaded a video he took with his GoPro to his social media. And a local news channel is going live with the footage now."

Stephenson leaned over Suarez's shoulder and ran a hand through his short blond hair. "Looks like Tess might get that closure she's been looking for," he said to his partner.

Suarez clicked on a video and the three detectives watched the underwater footage in silence. The visibility was surprisingly clear as the camera focused on the Lamborghini. The diver swam closer to the submerged vehicle. The driver's side door was opened at an upward angle. Stephenson felt a knot form in the back of his throat as the diver swam around the opened door and looked directly into the empty driver's seat.

"Oh, no," Stephenson heard himself say.

Adams shook his head. "There goes your honeymoon plans."

Stephenson and Adams sat across from Tess and Lieutenant Wallace in the conference room at the back of the Homicide Unit. While Stephenson appreciated his wife wasn't one to say, *I told you so,* he hated that he'd been wrong. And that he'd doubted her instincts.

"We've been monitoring Avery's bank accounts and credit cards," the lieutenant said. "And, although she was presumed dead, we still would've been alerted if she'd shown up on an airline passenger manifest or tried to leave the country."

"But," Tess continued, "Colton and Avery required many of EverChange's members to give up personal information, including bank account details, as an act of trust in the organization. So, it's possible Avery could be pulling money from a number of different accounts."

"*If* it's Avery," Stephenson said.

Tess locked eyes with him from across the table. "There's only one way to find out."

CHAPTER FORTY-FIVE

"I didn't realize the lake was this big." Stephenson looked out his passenger window. They'd been driving along the lake for nearly thirty minutes after passing through the town of Coeur d'Alene.

"Yeah, it's something like twenty-five miles long." Adams turned onto a private drive. "I used to come here as a kid."

Stephenson and Adams jumped out of their vehicle as soon as they came to a stop. Tess and four Idaho State SWAT detectives pulled up next to them and together they swiftly advanced to the lake home's front entrance with their weapons drawn.

A SWAT member tried the door handle. It didn't budge. He moved out of the way as another SWAT detective used both hands to swing a battering ram into the door.

The deadbolt broke away from the doorframe with a loud crack, and the door slammed into the adjacent wall. Pop music blared from the home's built-in speakers as they stepped inside, their guns aimed and ready.

"Police!"

Stephenson quickly swept the entry way and living room,

but both were empty. He used hand motions to show Adams he would follow SWAT to the left while Adams and Tess went with two other SWAT detectives to the right. Adams nodded, and he and Tess moved straight through the large living room.

Stephenson and the SWAT detectives led with their firearms as they moved silently down the pinewood paneled hallway. He recognized the Selena Gomez song that played through the house. They slowed when they reached an open doorway at the end of the hall. One of the SWAT detectives pivoted into the doorway in a swift motion.

"It's clear," she told him before stepping into the room.

The view out the empty bedroom was stunning. A few boats cruised past on the cobalt water. The late afternoon sun sank behind the evergreen trees across the lake.

Stephenson turned toward the movement out the sliding doors to his right. The afternoon breeze caught Avery's long blonde curls as she jumped from her lounge chair and ran across the patio in her tiny bikini.

Stephenson could hear Tess yelling above the music for her to stop when he opened the slider. Stephenson watched her disappear down a steep stairwell on the other side of an infinity pool as Tess and a SWAT detective ran after her.

Stephenson started after them but stopped when he spotted another set of stairs on his side of the pool. He sprinted toward them. When he got to the top, he saw the stairs met with the other staircase at the bottom and opened to a long floating dock.

He raced down the steep wooden stairs as fast as he could without taking a misstep. Avery had already reached the dock, and he watched her run toward a lone Jet Ski parked against the end of the floating structure. He was halfway down the stairs when Tess reached the bottom. She bolted down the dock after Avery.

Stephenson jumped over the last few steps onto the dock. He felt the SWAT detective right behind him as he chased after Tess. Avery had almost reached the Jet Ski when Tess closed the distance between them. Stephenson watched Tess holster her gun as Avery jumped onto the Jet Ski.

The Jet Ski's engine revved as Tess tackled Avery. Both women fell into the water as the Jet Ski flew forward. Stephenson ran to the edge of the dock where Tess and Avery had gone under. Stephenson couldn't see either of them beneath the sapphire lake. He was about to jump in when he heard them emerge from the water halfway back to shore.

He turned to see Tess had Avery in a headlock. They both gasped for air as Tess found her footing on the bottom of the lake and dragged Avery to shore. Avery's arms flailed as she tried unsuccessfully to break free of Tess's unrelenting hold.

Stephenson ran toward them and jumped into the shallow water when he reached the edge of the lake. Tess shoved Avery facedown onto the sand and pressed her knee into Avery's back. Tess finished securing Avery's second cuff behind her back when Stephenson reached them. It was clear she didn't need any help.

"Avery Hill," she said, "You're under arrest for the murders of Andrea Morris, Portia Grenalli, Summer Channing, and Colton Everett. You're also being charged with unlawful imprisonment of Portia Grenalli and Charity Green, reckless endangerment, sex trafficking, coercion, racketeering, and tax evasion."

Tess read Avery her Miranda rights as Adams and the other SWAT detectives looked on from the dock.

Avery cocked her head toward Stephenson. Her glare changed to a coy smile when she recognized him. When Tess finished, Avery looked beyond the thong of her bikini to meet Stephenson's gaze. "You miss me, Detective?"

Tess pulled Avery to her feet. "Let's go," she said, giving Avery's back a shove.

Avery kept her eyes on Stephenson as Tess led her past him and the other detectives.

"Guess you didn't need to get your shoes wet," Adams said with a smirk when Stephenson climbed back onto the dock.

When they reached the driveway, Tess helped Avery into the back of Stephenson's car.

"She's all yours," Tess said after closing the door.

"Good thing you came with us," he said.

She smiled. "You're welcome."

A half-hour later, Stephenson turned onto I-90. Tess followed behind them in her own unmarked Ford.

"I can't believe we went past The Coeur d'Alene Resort and didn't eat there," said Adams.

Stephenson glanced at Avery through his rearview mirror before he shot Adams a look. Sometimes, it was hard to tell when his partner was joking.

"What?" Adams shrugged his shoulders and watched the landscape rush by. "Their breaded trout is the best."

Tess walked out of their kitchen with a beer in each hand when Stephenson got home that night. After handing him one, she clinked their bottles together. He and Adams had booked Avery into jail after they'd returned from Coeur d'Alene. Her arraignment was scheduled for the next week.

"Cheers," she said before taking a drink.

"Cheers."

She took him by the hand and led him toward the living room couch.

He wrapped his arm around her as they took a seat. She leaned her head against his chest.

"I'm sorry for not opening up more to you about how Chris's murder was affecting me. I realize now that I wasn't even being honest with myself."

Since her time at the castle, she'd come to terms with her feelings over her brother's death. Surprisingly, by allowing herself to fully grieve Chris's murder, her anxiety had lifted. She also now had the peace of knowing his killer had been put away for life.

Stephenson pulled her closer. "It's okay. I should've been more aware of what you were going through.

"When this stuff with Avery is all over, we should go on a honeymoon. A real one. And I know the perfect place. But, if it's okay with you, I'd like to surprise you. Deal?"

"As long as I'm with you, I don't care where we go." She sat up and brought her face within inches of his. "As long as it's not Whidbey Island."

"Deal."

"I have a serious question for you."

"What?" he asked as Tess slid onto his lap.

"Do you want to be servant or master tonight?"

His lips formed a smile as she leaned her face closer to his.

"Um. I'm not sure," Stephenson said.

"I'm just kidding. I'm always the master."

Their laughter dissipated as he brought his mouth to hers.

WANT MORE?

Get your FREE bonus content and new release
updates at AUDREYJCOLE.COM/sign-up

EMERALD CITY THRILLERS
BY AUDREY J. COLE

THE RECIPIENT

INSPIRED BY MURDER

THE SUMMER NANNY

VIABLE HOSTAGE

FATAL DECEPTION

ABOUT THE AUTHOR

Audrey J. Cole is a registered nurse and a writer of thrillers set in Seattle. After living in Australia for five years, Audrey recently returned to the Pacific Northwest where she resides with her husband and two children.

Connect with Audrey:

f facebook.com/AudreyJCole

BB bookbub.com/authors/Audrey-J-Cole

instagram.com/AudreyJCole/

You can also visit her website:
www.AUDREYJCOLE.com

Manufactured by Amazon.ca
Bolton, ON

44812079R00173